THE RISE OF ALEC CALDWELL

Casey K. Cox hails from the West of England and dabbled in several genres before settling into m/m romance and erotica. Casey sees fiction as an adventure and a form of escape and has a wish to bring a touch of fantasy and a taste of the forbidden from the depths of the mind onto the page through the written word.

Casey K. Cox

The Rise of Alec Caldwell

Erotic Adventures of a Young Businessman

BRUNO GMÜNDER

The following is a work of homoerotic fiction. The Order of Gentlemen is a fictitious institution that exists only in this work of fiction. All characters are fictional. Any similarities with living or deceased people are completely coincidental. In case of real life events, creative license has been applied.

1st edition
© 2014 Bruno Gmünder Verlag GmbH
Kleiststraße 23-26, D-10787 Berlin
info@brunogmuender.com

© 2014 Casey K. Cox
Cover design: Steffen Kawelke
Cover photo: © menatplay.com
Printed in Germany

ISBN 978-3-86787-688-9

More about our books and authors:
www.brunogmuender.com

For Summer, Oli, and most definitely Roger

The Beginning—All in a Day's Work

Alexander Caldwell, better known to his few friends as Alec, stood beside the office water cooler. He gazed across the maze of paneled cubicles which filled the space before him, all occupied by small industrious groups. He could also see the odd gossipmonger here and there—those people who always had something to say about someone else. Apart from his friends, Tom Parsons and Chloe Fleming, Alec didn't get involved. He chose to mix only with his immediate team, and otherwise kept to himself as much as possible. There was a lot about Alec the gossips would avidly share, given the chance. The first would likely be the expression in his eyes whenever he was in the presence of Rick Hamilton. While half the office swooned and scraped at Hamilton's feet the man's effect on Alec was breathtakingly erotic.

Sadly, it was a hopeless cause. Exuding command and control, smart, sexy, and ridiculously successful for his age, Rick Hamilton could surely never be interested in the likes of Alec. Sure, Alec was good at his job, successful in his own right having secured a prestigious post as Senior Investment Manager at just twenty-four. But Hamilton…Hamilton couldn't have reached thirty and yet he had an entire floor of Seniors reporting to him and every one of them was just as talented, just as qualified as Alec. It would take Alec far more than six years to attain such a level, if indeed he ever would. Besides, there was no evidence Hamilton's sexual preference matched Alec's unexpressed desires. Why on earth would he need Alec? He probably had a hot supermodel girlfriend tucked away somewhere to hang on his every word. Alec was sure *he'd* hang on Hamilton's every vowel and consonant, if the man paid him enough attention. In a work capacity, Alec did have his ear to some extent because Rick Hamilton was Alec's line manager—cool, calm, and completely oblivious to Alec's crush.

Alec sighed. What he wouldn't give for a kiss from that man. Six feet of lightly muscled gorgeousness wrapped up in silky olive skin. His muscle definition showed up clearly through the close-fitted shirts he wore, to be peeked at on the rare occasions Hamilton removed his suit jacket. Fair hair—not blond, but definitely not mousey—framed his handsome face, from which shone blue eyes. Not a special kind of blue, just everyday blue, but to Alec they were still the bluest blue that cut through his calm and left him flustered whenever they came to rest on him.

A bit like right now, in fact. *Fuck! Caught staring again.* Third time in a week.

Hamilton smiled at him and Alec had to stifle a groan. God, did that man have any idea of the effect he had on him? He flushed as Hamilton continued to watch him. However much he wanted to, Alec couldn't look away. Those blue eyes seemed to undress him as they scanned his body and returned to his face with another quirk of the beautiful lips. If Hamilton kept staring, Alec would embarrass himself by shooting a load right there at the water cooler, full cup still in his hand. Definite cock swell happening.

The thought was enough to shake him out of his daydream. He chugged back the water, and high-tailed it to the bathroom.

Fuck, what an idiot. A stupid... pathetic... virgin... idiot. Perhaps if the last part hadn't been true he'd have had the courage to talk to his boss a little, gauge whether he could be interested. But what was the point? It wasn't as though Alec knew what to do with any man let alone Hamilton, should the heavens grant him a miracle and Hamilton appear interested. Alec Caldwell: investment manager for a large, respectable corporation; and twenty-four year old virgin. He'd had plenty of opportunities but none that appealed enough to push him through the barrier into manhood. He was obviously defective.

But he didn't feel defective, locked in a toilet stall, jerking off to the image of those everyday blue eyes cutting through his layer of cool. Right now, he felt every tug on his never-used-for-its-purpose, rock-hard cock. His hand braced against the cherry wood partition and he opened his mouth with a silent cry as he came into the apron of tissue covering his knees.

Yes, Alec Caldwell was a pathetic, virgin, idiot indeed.

Perhaps he should pay a hooker to show him the ropes. But that wouldn't work. He'd tried a few times with that idea but could never carry it through. This time would likely be no different. He lacked conviction. He had always been terrible at making decisions about his personal life. What he needed was a miracle of some description, at the very least a knight in shining armor to take the reins and lead the way.

Oh well. Back to work.

On the Job Training

Alec listened as Chloe reeled off the latest conquest in her *fuck every man in a fifty-mile radius* life goal. Josh, Alec heard her say, was thirty-two and married but his wife didn't like sex now she'd had their first child. Poor Josh had to make do with once a month—*if,* he was lucky. That sounded more than lucky from Alec's corner. The words floated through his brain initiating auto-response as his mind focused on the curve of Rick Hamilton's ass where he leaned over Sophie's shoulder at the desk behind Chloe. Alec's eye slowly traced the line over the hip and shoulder to—*fuck...* Hamilton was looking at him. Alec flushed at the smile playing over Hamilton's lips and concentrated on Chloe, concentrated so hard that when Hamilton touched his shoulder, he jumped almost a foot in the air.

"I'd like to see you in my office, Alec."

"Yes, sir. Now?"

"I think so, yes."

Damn and blast. Alec tidied a few things on his desk and made his way to Hamilton's office. He blushed as he closed the door and stood before the desk. Alec tried to fill his mind with mundane things—*the sky looked gray for the time of the afternoon, maybe it would rain. The cherry color of Hamilton's office furniture was the same as that of the toilet cubicle where Alec...* not such a good train of thought. Alec coughed lightly, trying to shake the idea of jerking off to the image of Hamilton's face out of his mind.

"No need to stand on ceremony. Take a seat."

"Thank you, sir."

"How long have you been here, Alec?"

"Two years, sir. Ten months on your team."

"Do you like it here?"

"Very much."

"And why is that?"

Was it a trick question? Was he expecting Alec to own up to the fact it was because he liked staring at Hamilton's butt? "The salary is good, the people are friendly and I enjoy my work."

"I may have something else for you."

Fuck, no. Hamilton was going to transfer him out of the department. Alec's shoulders slumped and his hands gripped the arms of the leather chair as he shuffled uncomfortably in his seat. Get rid of the embarrassing coworker with a crush. What else would it be?

"You'll continue with your present workload. This will be along the lines of additional duties. Do you think you would be interested?"

No transfer. "Absolutely, sir. I'm very keen to increase my experience within the company."

"Hmm. Stand up, Alec, and come here." Hamilton swivelled his chair to the side and gestured to the space directly in front of him.

Alec did as he was told, trying not to pass out cold as he met Hamilton's gaze. Looking down into Hamilton's face definitely made Alec feel giddy. If only he had the courage to reach out and touch.

"You're a sweet boy, Alec. Something tells me you haven't quite understood what I'm offering you."

"A chance for additional duties, reporting directly to you, sir?" *Maybe, I think.* No, Alec didn't have a clue. What other possibilities were there?

Hamilton stood up and walked behind him. Alec could feel his breath so close to his neck, his cock started to swell. *Think of something else. Think of anything else.*

"It would mean late nights, working over your lunch hour and reporting to me personally every day." The hot breath curled into Alec's brain. "Will that be a problem?"

"Not at all, sir." *Not in a million fucking years would spending more time with you be a problem.*

Hamilton returned to his desk and picked up a piece of paper. "There will, of course, be a pay increase to reflect the extra duties. Will this be sufficient?" He handed Alec the paper.

Fucking hells bells. An extra twenty thousand a year. *Twenty-fucking-grand.*

"M-more than sufficient, sir. Thank you." Alec placed the paper back on the desk.

Restlessly, Hamilton prowled around behind him again and pressed his chin to Alec's shoulder. His hand swept lightly over Alec's arm to his shoulder and Alec shuddered, his body responding without his permission. Hamilton's words came breathily quiet in Alec's ear. "But you don't know what the duties involve. How do you know if it's enough?"

"Oh, well, um…" Nope. Alec couldn't get the words out with Hamilton so close. It was difficult to breathe or keep hold of any thought other than if he were to turn his head, his lips would brush Hamilton's cheek. Rock hard cock. *Fuck, fuck, fuck.*

"You look uncomfortable. Let me take your jacket." Hamilton's arms slid around Alec's waist and opened the button. He slipped the suit coat off Alec's shoulders. Nothing left to hide the erection straining against his pants now. Hamilton folded Alec's jacket over the desk and stood in front of him. "You seem to have a problem," he smiled, tracing light fingers over Alec's cock. Alec shuddered again. He'd blow any second. How more pathetic could he be?

12

"I'm *so* sorry, Mr. Hamilton." Alec closed his eyes and looked at the floor. *Just shoot me already.*

"Nothing to be ashamed of, Alec. I like that you find me attractive."

"I do. I mean, you do?"

Hamilton chuckled, still stroking the line of Alec's cock. "Oh, yes. It will help tremendously. It will ensure your new duties are much more pleasant."

"It will?"

Hooking a hand in the waistband of Alec's pants, Hamilton tugged him closer before sitting in his chair. He studied Alec again with those damn sexy eyes. Alec missed his touch. How fucking stupid was that? Shouldn't he be thinking of sexual harassment? His boss had touched him up. But what did Alec expect when he was the one always making eyes at Hamilton?

"Let me help you out with that." Hamilton wheeled forward in his chair and reached out to unbuckle Alec's belt.

You have got to be kidding me.

Hamilton unhooked Alec's pants, pulled the zipper and let them drop to the floor. Alec could only stare, open mouthed, as Hamilton kneaded his cock through his underwear. Hamilton winked at him as he pulled at the waistband and slipped his hands into Alec's shorts, pulling them free of his erection and sliding them down to meet his pants. *Holy, fucking, moly.*

"Everything okay so far?" Hamilton said.

"Uh… oh, absolutely, Mr. Hamilton, sir."

"Good. Then we understand each other."

I don't understand a fucking thing but I am not complaining—oh no, not me.

Hamilton watched Alec's face as he leaned forward and licked a drop of pre-come from the head of Alec's cock. Alec groaned loudly

13

and Hamilton chuckled before taking the whole head into his mouth and sucking.

"Oh. Sweet, lord. I'll come in about five seconds."

Hamilton pulled back, letting Alec's cock slip from his lips and took up a steady stroking motion with his hand as he watched Alec's face.

"I'll make a mess," Alec said, squirming on the spot but not wanting it to stop.

"Yes, it does tend to do that." Hamilton let go and sat back. "Do you suck cock, Alec?"

"Do I, uh…no, sir. I never have before."

"But you'd like to, you like men?"

"Yes, sir. I'm happy to have a go. For you, I mean. I'm willing to learn."

"You are a strange one." Hamilton picked up his cell phone and appeared to send a text. He put it back on the desk and looked at Alec. "Take off your shoes and pants and bend over the desk."

Fuck. This was *it*. Hamilton was going to pop his cherry. Alec couldn't believe his body was complying with the instructions without his mind engaging. It had always been the other way around: Alec desperate to follow through but his body wouldn't move. Now, in an office where anyone could walk in, he was half-naked so his boss could play with him, and everything seemed to be working. Was the risk of being caught the key all along, or was it the authority in Hamilton's voice that pushed him into motion? Alec realized he couldn't care less, he was just glad it was happening. It brought a whole new meaning to the phrase "being caught with your pants down."

"Good boy," Hamilton said as Alec bent over and held the edge of the desk. The words went straight to Alec's cock and it jumped obediently. Alec heard the squeak of desk chair wheels on the floor behind him. Soft hands kneaded Alec's butt cheeks before prying them open. A tongue lapped over his hole and he jerked. "Everything okay?" Hamilton asked.

"Yes, I just wasn't expecting it." *Why would I think my boss was going to lick my ass? For fuck's sake.*

"Should I use lube instead?"

Damn. He was going to lose the opportunity of his life and all because he was a useless waste of a space virgin. He should lie. Just say *yes* and let the man get on with it.

"Are you sure you're okay with this, Alec?" Hamilton's hand smoothing over his back was the last straw.

"I'm so sorry, Mr. Hamilton." Alec was close to tears. Desperately trying to hold on to a last scrap of dignity seemed silly in his current position, but he really didn't want to cry. "I've never. It's just that… I don't know what to do."

"You've never been taken before?"

"No, sir."

"That's okay, what do you do for your boyfriends?"

Alec felt completely stupid. There was no point lying, he was rubbish at keeping up pretence. Better to just tell the truth and get it over with. "If you want to replace me, sir, I understand. I'm sorry I'm not suitable."

"You've never had anal sex?"

"I've never had *any* kind of sex. Period, sir."

"I'm sorry, Alec, are you telling me you're a virgin? As in, a God's honest truth, pure-as-the-driven-snow kind of virgin?"

Alec couldn't hold the pose anymore; he turned, fell to his knees in front of Hamilton, and reached for his hand. "Please, Mr. Hamilton. I want to do this with you, for you. I want you to fuck me. I know I'm stupid and pathetic, but I fancy you like crazy and you're the first person to suck my cock, so it makes sense for you to be the first to fuck me. I—"

"Stop." Hamilton seemed to be thinking. He stroked Alec's hair and face and Alec moved into the touch. It felt so natural. "I won't fuck you." Alec dropped his forehead on to Hamilton's knee. Now he wanted to cry but the tears were stuck. "Not today anyway." Alec looked up at him. Was that a glimmer of hope? "Your first time should be special, Alec, not over the desk at work."

"But you will?"

"Yes, of course. I'm honored, really. Beautiful thing like you falling at my feet and pleading, how could I refuse?" Alec gasped lightly at Hamilton's smile. "So sweet," Hamilton said, and reached forward to touch Alec's lips with his.

Alec curled a hand around Hamilton's neck and pulled him into a full kiss. That, at least, he knew how to do. He groaned as Hamilton's tongue slipped into his mouth and he returned his own, searching out his taste. Incredible. Everything he'd thought it would be. Alec's cock bounced back to attention and he stroked it while deepening the kiss.

Hamilton pulled back, his eyes sparkling. "Wow, you seem to have mastered that very well." He noticed Alec's hand and slapped it away. "You don't touch unless you're given permission."

"Sorry, sir. I don't know the rules. Will you teach me? Make me what you need me to be."

"Bend over the desk again. I'll start to open you up a little."

Alec was more confident this time. Hamilton knew the truth and still wanted this, still wanted him. That had to count for something. Hamilton spread his cheeks and licked and kissed his pucker.

"You must tell me if I do anything you don't like or if I hurt you."

"Yes, sir. All good, so far." The sound was throaty. Hamilton was already licking and sucking over his hole again and then *fucking halle-lujah*, his tongue pushed straight inside Alec's ass. He was clean, wasn't he? Of course he was clean, he always kept meticulously clean. But was it clean enough? There were no complaints, so Alec relaxed into the sensations. His knees buckled and Hamilton let out a short laugh as he propped up Alec's hips while still fucking him with his tongue. Alec rocked gently back against him, imagining a cock there instead.

He'd always wanted to shove something up his ass when he jacked off but never found the courage. He always wanted to watch gay porn but was too afraid the police would come knocking on his door, even though it seemed everyone watched endless porn online these days. But now... now, Hamilton was personally inducting him into the sex club. It was such a weight off his mind knowing he wouldn't die a virgin because of his indecision. Hamilton didn't love him but he was obviously into him and that was more than enough. Hamilton also seemed to know exactly what Alec wanted and that made Alec's job easy. He just had to do whatever he was told to do. The thought sent a sudden, unexpected rush to his cock. "I'm going to come," he mumbled. Hamilton stopped. "No, don't stop. Please." But the moment passed and Alec's breathing started to settle.

"First lesson, Alec, you don't come until I tell you."

"I'll try not to but—"

"No buts. If you come before I say, you will be punished. Do you understand?"

Punished? What the fuck? Alec tried to gather a few thoughts together.

"Alec, do you want to learn the rules or not?"

Rules. Rules were good. Alec could follow rules. Rules kept him safe. Rules were his life. "Yes. I'm not to come, until you say."

Hamilton stroked a hand over Alec's back. "Good boy." Pre-come seeped from the tip of his cock at those words. "I'm going to fuck you with my fingers. Just relax and try not to clench." Hamilton rummaged in a desk drawer. A moment later, a slick finger slipped through Alec's pucker into his ass. Not uncomfortable but an odd sensation. Was that all there was to being fucked? What on earth was the fuss about? A steady rhythm started and again Alec rocked into the motion. "Good boy," Hamilton purred. "You're a natural. Just stay nice and relaxed."

Oh, fuck. Alec's knees buckled again as Hamilton hit something.

"Say hello to your prostate, Alec. The reason even straight men are known to like a finger fuck."

"I can see why. Oh, shit, I'm going to come. I won't be able to stop it."

Hamilton stood quickly and Alec jumped as Hamilton slapped hard over his ass. Another blow, surprisingly painful, made Alec flinch. "Do I need to continue?"

"No, sir. I'm sorry. I'll try harder." Harder was the right word. His cock was bordering on painful, but that stung, and wasn't fun. Not really. Maybe a little. But he had other things to concentrate on right now.

Hamilton resumed his position and continued to fuck him, this time with two fingers. Good, it felt very good. Alec was trying to think of random things, willing away his erection when the door opened. Someone came in and the door closed softly. Alec heard it lock. *Fucking hell!*

Hamilton didn't stop. Alec kept his head down.

"Mr. Hamilton, sir."

Holy hell, it's Michael. Michael from the second floor. Despite the fact a colleague was witnessing him being finger fucked by his line manager, Alec couldn't stop the gentle rocking motion Hamilton's action caused in his body.

Hamilton smoothed over Alec's back in that reassuring way he was starting to like. "Good boy, Alec. This is Michael. Strip, Michael. He's another one of my boys, Alec."

Not just Alec then. No wonder all this seemed so normal to Hamilton. Did Alec care? Hell, no. He twisted sideways enough to see

Hamilton's fingers disappear inside him. It was the hottest thing he'd ever seen. He saw a naked Michael, with an impressive semi-hard cock, kneel at Hamilton's feet and lean forward to kiss his shoe. Alec was too close and desperately fighting his orgasm to have thoughts about it. The relentless rhythm was threatening to carry him away.

"Suck Alec's cock, Michael. We want this to be a day he remembers for a very long time."

Michael crawled underneath Alec and sucked in his entire length. Alec whimpered. "Please, I can't, oh god, please."

Hamilton thrust faster with his fingers, stroking Alec's back steadily. Michael was doing clever things with his tongue that ate away at Alec's brain, eroding his composure. His whole body trembled with the strain of not coming. *Don't come, don't come, don't come.* "Please, Mr. Hamilton, please. I want to be a good boy but it's so hard. I'm so close. I want to be good. Fuck, fuck, *fuck.*" Hamilton thrust deeper and faster, rubbing over that spot as Michael sucked harder.

"Come for me, Alec."

"Oh, fuck *yes.*" Alec sprayed into Michael's throat. On and on it came, his body clenching around Hamilton's fingers. He rested his head on his arm and panted. His shirt stuck to his back, sticky with sweat. Michael licked over the head of Alec's cock one more time then took up his position at Hamilton's feet.

"Very well done, Alec. You came on command first time. I'm very pleased with you."

"T-thank you... sir."

"Now take off your shirt and come here. Michael is going to teach you how to suck cock."

Interesting on-the-job training, Alec thought, as he stripped off the sweaty shirt and rubbed the cum into his belly. He caught a glimpse of himself in the large mirrored cabinet against the wall looking flushed and sated, and quirked a smile before taking up a position on his knees next to Michael. Hamilton stroked Alec's cheek and sat back in his chair. Every second of attention from Hamilton did things to Alec's insides. He had the strange urge to climb onto his lap and curl against his chest. No time to think about that now.

The lesson began. Michael took out Hamilton's cock. He demonstrated teasing the tip with his tongue and then sat back. Alec looked at Hamilton who motioned him forward. Alec took hold of Hamilton's cock with a small contented sigh and stroked it. *Magnificent.* His daydreams had never taken him this far. Hamilton's cock, waiting for Alec's attention, did it get any better than this? He leaned in to kiss the tip, tasting salty pre-come on his lips, and he licked them slowly before copying the tease Michael had showed him. He kissed the head again and—for good measure and because he could—he sucked the end into his mouth. It tasted amazing. His tongue swirled around the head and he groaned softly, sucking once more before he let it go and sat back. No good, he couldn't leave it alone. He reached forward once more to kiss it again.

"Are you sure you need me?" Michael chuckled. Alec blushed and Hamilton took hold of his chin and pulled him up for a kiss. Alec threw himself into that kiss letting his hands wander and stroke Hamilton's cock.

"I can't believe it," Alec said, when Hamilton broke away. "I can't believe I get to touch you and kiss you." Alec dipped his head for another quick kiss and suck of Hamilton's cock before sitting back to await instruction.

"You are the most incredibly beautiful thing," Hamilton said. He stroked Alec's cheek again. "My beautiful boy."

Alec smiled. He liked that a lot. *Hamilton's beautiful boy.*

The lesson continued. He didn't do too badly and he certainly enjoyed himself. He sat back and watched as Michael finished the job and swallowed Hamilton's load. When Michael came up for air there was a small drop on his lip. Alec wanted to taste it. He wiped it away with his thumb and licked it off.

"Do you like it?" Hamilton smiled broadly.

"Very much." Alec grinned. "Is there anymore?"

Hamilton roared with laughter. "You are remarkable and hard again, I see." Alec went to stroke his cock but remembered he wasn't allowed to touch and dropped his hand. "Good boy. I think you deserve a little something special."

More special than the orgasm of a lifetime *and* getting to suck Hamilton's cock? Maybe Hamilton was going to fuck him after all. Alec certainly felt like he needed something up his ass right now.

"Michael, present yourself for our boy." Michael spun around on his knees and leaned forward placing his chest and shoulders against the floor. He opened his legs slightly and spread his ass cheeks.

Fuck, that is hot. Alec's cock was as eager to get to work as he was.

"You're going to fuck him for me, Alec."

"I don't know how."

"I'll guide you." Hamilton grabbed the lube and a condom. "Kneel between his legs." Alec followed the instruction. His cock bounced along Michael's crack and the pucker spasmed. Hamilton knelt behind Alec and wrapped his arms around his waist. He leaned his chin on one shoulder so he could see to unroll a condom over Alec's cock. Then he spread lube all over it. "Hold out two fingers." Hamilton poured a small amount of lube on Alec's fingers. "Now push them slowly inside, like I did with you." Alec rubbed over Michael's pucker a few times and pushed past the tight ring all the way in and back out.

He repeated the process and Michael started to moan. "Good boy, Alec," Hamilton whispered in his ear. "Very good. Do you like to be a good boy?"

"Yes. I like being your good boy, sir." Alec turned to capture Hamilton's lips while still finger fucking Michael. *So erotic.* He was certainly making up for lost time and being told what to do made everything easy. No stress, no mistakes to make. He was free to enjoy the process.

Hamilton kissed over his cheek as Alec looked back to see his fingers disappearing into Michael. *Incredible.* Why had he thought this would be so difficult?

"That's enough." Hamilton placed a hand around Alec's cock and lined it up with Michael's hole, leaning against him from behind a little to move his hips. "I'm going to fuck Michael using your cock, Alec. Is that okay?"

"Use me as you see fit, sir."

"God, you are so damn hot," Hamilton said. He bit down on Alec's shoulder and pushed forward so that Alec's cock slipped past the sphincter ring and into Michael up to the hilt.

"Fuck," Alec gasped. "It's so tight. I can't, oh…"

"Just rest there until it passes." Hamilton kissed his neck and shoulders. "You're no longer a virgin, Alec," he whispered. "And tomorrow I will take you home and make love to you all night long, until all thoughts of virginity are banished from your mind and all that's left is me."

"Hell, yes." Alec started to move and Hamilton held his hips, rocking back and forth with him. Michael seemed to disappear and all that remained was Hamilton moving Alec's body, Hamilton whispering sweet nothings, Hamilton kissing and stroking and pumping him faster and faster, stealing his mind and his thoughts and claiming his soul.

"Stand up, Alec." Hamilton sat back in his chair and pulled Alec to him. Stripping away the condom, he took in Alec's whole length and sucked. Michael knelt at Alec's feet and Alec stroked his hair. He held Michael by the shoulder, pulled him close so his cheek rubbed against Alec's thigh, so close to where Hamilton worked over Alec's cock. Hamilton stoked the heat pooling in Alec's guts and drove him closer to the edge. He let the cock slip out of his mouth and smiled up at him. "Come for me, Alec." he said, and opened his mouth. It was more than Alec could cope with. He let go and erupted a fountain of cum over Hamilton's face and lips. Hamilton sucked him back in and swallowed the rest, licking and cleaning before finally letting go. He wiped over his face and smiled. "It's very good for the skin. Now, I think Michael deserves a little something. Suck him until he comes, Alec, and make sure you swallow it all."

From virgin to two cocks in one sitting, Alec thought, as he sucked Michael's cock with the techniques he'd just learned. But this wasn't really for Michael. This was for Hamilton. It may as well have been Hamilton's cock and Alec was extremely pleased with himself as he felt the warm liquid spill over his tongue. He lost most of it as it dribbled over his chin, but he did swallow. Not a bad taste. Not as good as Hamilton's.

"Oh, bravo." Hamilton clapped and pulled Alec in for a kiss to share the cum around his lips. "Definitely a natural. I am going to have so much fun with you."

"I hope so, Mr. Hamilton. It's certainly been fun for me."

Hamilton slapped his ass playfully. "Get dressed both of you and head back to work. Alec, I'll see you first thing in the morning please."

"Yes, sir, thank you."

That evening Alec jerked off in the shower to the sound of Hamilton's voice in his ear, to the feel of Hamilton's hand stroking his back and the sensation of Hamilton's fingers thrusting inside him. Overall, Alec decided it was a very satisfactory promotion indeed.

Breakfast Meeting

"Good morning, Alec. I do believe you're early."

Alec grinned as he closed the door and stood in front of Hamilton's desk. "I was anxious to get started with my extra duties, sir."

"Very well, lock the door and strip."

So easy to follow orders. As Alec folded his clothes neatly and made his way to kneel at Hamilton's feet, he was interested to see his cock already hard. He leaned forward and kissed Hamilton's shoe as he'd seen Michael do the day before. He was surprised at how right, how natural it felt.

"You pick things up quickly, well done."

"My aim is to please you, sir." And wasn't that true. Alec had thought of nothing else all morning than how to be the best office boy so that Hamilton would want to keep him. Then perhaps kiss him, touch him, and fuck him into tomorrow for the next ten years and into forever.

"Yes, we'll discuss more of that over the coming week. This is a trial position. If at any time you are asked to do something you're not happy with, you should tell me immediately. You have to be a willing participant, Alec. Do you understand?"

"I understand."

"You can ask me anything. I'm particularly interested in how you feel about what I ask you to do and what it does for you. Everything is up for discussion. You are still my employee but I hope we will also become friends."

"I would like that very much." *Seeing as you're going to be fucking me on a regular basis and offering me around.* The unreality of the situation was beginning to dawn. It wasn't uncomfortable. Just…odd.

"Do you have any questions?"

Where to start? Alec had so many questions it was difficult to prioritise them. He was sure Hamilton would only allow a few at a time. He thought for a moment. "What actually is Michael's role, my role?"

"At its core this company has a very unusual structure. It stretches across many companies of note throughout the city. Your official title will come later, for now think of it as a club with extra-curricular activities. In your capacity, you must be very discreet and discuss it only with those I introduce you to. Do you understand?"

"Absolutely."

"One of the functions of the club is to provide entertainment for clients, visiting members from other organizations and offices."

Alec felt his shoulders drop. He was being trained as a whore…a business perk.

Hamilton lifted Alec's chin with a finger to regain eye contact. "Don't look that way. You hold a very respectable position in this company that you obtained through your own merit. This position is a reward. Once you have served as an office boy, many doors will open for you. You will meet very influential people, men and women who can make things happen."

"I'll be required to serve women?" Fuck, he was only just getting to grips with what to do with a man and he didn't like the idea of catering to women that way. He'd never keep his cock hard for all those soft wobbly bits.

"As you've openly expressed your sexuality, that won't be necessary. Most of the clientele are gentleman wanting the services of a young man during their stay. Not all our boys are naturally inclined although they make exceptions for the long-term benefits. There's no shortage of volunteers for the few female clients we serve."

"What happens when an office boy isn't a boy anymore?"

Hamilton paused in thought, cocking his head slightly to one side as though weighing Alec through his words. "We don't throw you out, if that's what you're asking. Most serve only for a few years through their own choice. They find a partner; want to settle into a regular life. You retain all financial benefits and there is usually a further promotion when your term comes to an end."

That all sounded fair enough. Maybe he could drop the office boy fucking and sucking after a few years and just stay with Hamilton. *If,* Hamilton wanted him.

"Why did you choose me?"

Hamilton reached out and pulled Alec to him. He kissed his face all over and ran his hands through Alec's hair. "You are a personal weakness. I've seen you watching me and I wanted you. It's as simple as that."

Alec let the revelation settle in. Hamilton wanted him. Hamilton, the unattainable ironclad god of the eighth floor wanted *him*. A shudder of pleasure ran through Alec's body from head to toe and Hamilton kissed him again.

It was a good answer. Alec liked that answer a lot. In fact, it was the most incredible thing he had ever heard. Although, not actually having had sex yet, he wasn't sure he was going to want to be fucked by a dozen other office boys and every guy with a club membership. "But you'll offer me to clients, like you gave Michael to me yesterday?"

Hamilton dropped his hand from Alec's cheek and Alec found himself moving toward it instinctively, missing the touch, and wanting more. "No. I've decided not to do that with you, due to your unusual circumstances."

"My virginity."

"Yes. You asked me to be your first and I will. But you need time to adjust and think about your own needs. I will expect you to fuck others, but until such time as you're ready, only I will fuck you."

Hell's bloody bells. For once, his lack of sexual experience had earned him a bonus instead of relegating him to the bottom of the heap. Perfect answer. Exactly what he wanted. "Thank you, so much." Alec fell and kissed Hamilton's feet.

"You're very welcome." Hamilton smoothed a hand over Alec's head and pulled him into another heated kiss.

A new future blazed bright in Alec's mind where his days consisted of hours of hot sex and long lingering kisses. And cocks, he supposed, of random clients picked out of a hat. Alec pulled back from the kiss.

"What about diseases, STD's…and stuff. I sucked Michael without a condom. I could still catch something right, from blowjobs, from swallowing?"

"Very good question." Hamilton straightened his tie in a very business-like fashion and Alec wished he'd let the kissing carrying on instead. "I'm pleased you thought to ask. Safety is of the utmost importance, both of the boys and the clients. As a boy, you will undergo regular health screening and will only be on active duty with an all clear. The same applies to the client. If they wish to make use of member services they have to hold up to date health certificates. We have our own health clinics to ensure standards and privacy."

Hamilton reached for his wallet and pulled out a card. He handed it to Alec. "Normally you would be asked to undergo the medical prior to starting work but given your situation…"

Alec looked at the card. There was a small logo in the top right hand corner that resembled a coat of arms, a valid from and to date, and a statement in bold print across the centre—Cleared for access to all services.

Hamilton took the card and put it back in his wallet. "I suppose I shouldn't assume you have an all clear because of your lack of experience." He smiled reassuringly. "I'll book the tests for later today. You can always ask to see a member's card before you service. Any late tests or issues are flagged to service managers immediately, but you are within your rights to ask, regardless."

"That's good to know."

"Any more questions?"

"I think that's everything for now." Alec sat back on his heels and gazed up at Hamilton. *He has the pick of all the office boys out there but he wanted me.* Alec grinned and a happy sigh escaped his lips.

There was a definite reaction in Hamilton's trousers as he looked Alec over. "I have a soft spot for you already, Alec. I'm so pleased you're taking to this so well. Now, show me what you remember of sucking cock. I've been thinking of nothing else since you left yesterday. I want to see your lips wrapped around me again."

Funny, pretty much the same as Alec had been thinking. He was happy to oblige. He lost his rhythm a few times as his own desire spiked, but he remembered to keep up the pressure and alternate the speed. He listened for the sounds that showed him when he did something Hamilton particularly liked. Those things he would definitely remember. In the end it got the better of him and he let go. He lavished all his attention on worshiping the cock, which fit so well into his hand and tasted so right in his mouth. His reward was the bittersweet flavor of Hamilton's cum running down his throat. This time he didn't spill a drop.

Alec let the cock soften in his mouth not wanting to let it go but he did when Hamilton cupped his chin. "Thank you, beautiful." Hamilton smiled and Alec's heart skipped. He felt like a puppy desperate for the slightest word of recognition from its master. "Now bend over the desk and let me give you your reward."

Alec moaned and groaned and squealed and puffed as Hamilton fucked him thoroughly with three twisting digits. It took all his will power not to spill with every thrust that hit that place and it seemed Hamilton knew exactly where it was. Just as he was losing all sense of self, Hamilton pulled him around and sucked down hard. Alec staggered back against the desk, incoherent babbling falling from his lips, the determination not to climax disintegrating with every clever swirl of Hamilton's tongue. And then it stopped. Alec almost reached out to hold Hamilton's head and thrust into that teasing throat.

"Very well done, Alec. Now, get dressed and go to work."

"What? You can't leave me like this."

"I can and I will. Consider it part of your training. Under no circumstances do you touch yourself during office hours, unless I give you permission."

"But—"

"I know you used to sneak off to the bathrooms. Now, tell me you understand."

So not fucking fair. "Yes, sir."

"Don't be despondent. I promise I'll make it up to you this evening. You'll come to my apartment and sleep over. I'm having a party. It'll be a good chance for you to see that there are other opportunities available."

Alec dressed quietly and straightened his tie. His cock was uncomfortable trapped in his tight shorts and his balls were fit to burst. But he'd had a little time to think. "You don't have to make anything up to me, sir," he said, once he was ready. "I'll gladly do whatever's required for my training. Even, if it means sitting at my desk with the boner from hell."

"You are just incredible. Come here so I can kiss you."

Definitely not so bad, after all.

Welcome Party

Alec bounded down the stairs from his apartment. He was so excited to be heading to Hamilton's place, his actual house, *and* be sleeping over. The evening promised special things—his cherry finally popped in every way and years of mind-blowing orgasms and hot office sex to follow. His life had gone from boring and unfulfilled to totally amazing in two days.

His cock had been at varying degrees of hardness all day, never fully softening. Hamilton had called him in at lunchtime; finger fucked him to frenzy and then let him give a slow, sloppy blowjob that left his belly full of Hamilton. Before he'd left for home, he sucked Hamilton again and almost died of frustration from a teasing tongue fuck. He still hadn't been allowed to come.

Hamilton let him slide close in the back of the car. They kissed a little and Hamilton held his hand. "Are you nervous?"

"Hardly, I can't wait." Alec grinned and leaned in for another kiss.

"There are some things I need to explain, Alec."

"I'm ready."

"I live life a little differently. I suppose you could say I'm more entrenched in the Gentleman's Club I spoke of than many you'll meet. I don't have a wife and children in the country."

"You're still young."

"I don't intend to follow that route. I'm not an opportunist, Alec.

I'm gay. Thankfully, I don't need to project a particular image and I can indulge my eccentricities."

"And that means?"

"It means that I choose to keep houseboys as well as office boys."

"Newbie virgin here, remember? You're going to have to explain slowly."

Hamilton chuckled and pulled him in for a squeeze. "I'm a master at home. I have three slave boys that live with me during the weekends."

"Three?"

"I get very hungry." He smiled. "Actually, I keep three because I hold parties that cater for a particular scene and I frequent certain clubs where my boys are offered for service."

"They're whores?"

"No. I can understand why you would think that but they aren't paid for sex. I'm hoping seeing it in action will help you to understand how it works."

"And what will I be doing tonight?"

"You will stay with me. Ask as many questions as you need to. Meet my guests and, of course, my boys."

"And I'm here as an extension of work rather than a guest?"

"Both. You are my guest so that we can get to know each other and you are also in training for your new position."

"I understand." If Hamilton said strip and suck that's what he'd do. If he said bend over and eventually at some point come—he would do that too, even in front of a room full of people. And he didn't have to worry about an Alec fucking frenzy, because for now, Hamilton was keeping him for his sole use. In the meantime, he would get to watch lots of sex and maybe fuck a boy or two. Sounded like fun.

"When you say, *boy*?"

"Don't worry. I never use anyone under twenty at the parties or clubs. I like my boys to be men who know what they want rather than

31

confused kids that haven't had time to discover their own needs. Do you like young boys?"

"No. I was just curious. I wouldn't have been comfortable watching that."

"It's good to know we agree on that, at least. I urge you to refrain from getting involved in discussions concerning age of consent. Some of my guests have very different views."

"I see."

"Alec, I don't mean they fuck children. Our club doesn't condone that. But the legal age for sex in this country is sixteen. For me a sixteen-year-old is still too young to understand the concept of being a houseboy. But some of the men and women you will meet over the next year do not agree with me."

Alec thought for a moment... There were lines he knew he would never cross, even for the ongoing attentions in what was amounting to a brave, yet bizarre, new world. He was relieved to know Hamilton, at least, was on the same side of those very important lines.

"You should also know that many of the houseboys and those at clubs are chosen because they look very young for their age. You'll understand what I mean when you meet Sebastian."

"You chose him for that reason?"

"No, he chose me, but he's a good example of the men you will meet who serve outside the office."

That served in ways Alec didn't have to for the moment. "Will I be one of your houseboys?"

"Only you can decide if that's what you want. For now, take note of how they behave and react to what's going on around them. Now, the party started before I came to collect you. The boys will already be in action. There's no stopping them once they get going."

Hamilton grinned and Alec caught a twinkle of mischief in his eye that went straight to his cock. That and the thought of walking in on a room of full of hot bodies and even hotter sex made Alec's trousers tight. He shifted uncomfortably.

"I'm not doing too badly for someone who's never even watched a porn movie. I seem to have found the fast track."

"Oh god, everything you say just makes me want to kiss you."

Alec grinned. "I'm not stopping you."

Hamilton was practically humping Alec's hip by the time they pulled up outside the apartment block. "You drive me crazy, Alec. I can't wait till I get my cock in that delicious ass of yours and make you mine."

Make you mine. Alec liked the sound of that. A lot. Even more than 'I wanted you'.

By the time they were in the elevator, Alec was feeling a little intimidated. The building was huge with a concierge at reception who had opened the door for them like they did in movies. Not only did Alec feel out of place as the only virgin at the sex party, he'd wandered into territory well above his pay grade.

Hamilton saw his concerned look. "You'll be brilliant Alec. I have great faith in you." Hamilton kissed his cheek and opened the door.

Contemporary art lined the walls of the long, wide hall that opened before them. As the door closed softly and they stepped farther inside, the unmistakable grunts and groans of sex could be heard coming from up ahead. Hamilton took Alec's jacket and hung it with his own in a closet to the left. He placed his keys on a smoky mirrored console table that reflected the muted color from the walls, and took Alec's hand.

"Still okay?"

Alec took a deep breath. "Yes. I'll be okay as long as you're close."

"Good boy."

Alec followed Hamilton along the extravagant hallway to the first doorway. None of the chat in the ride over had prepared him for the mind-blowing sight which greeted his eyes as they stepped through the open double-doors. Alec didn't know where to look first: was it the huge scale of the living room, which looked be at least sixty feet long, and variously furnished in different sections; or was it the rampant sex? With so many naked bodies writhing over the lush furniture, Alec couldn't discern the various areas' functions in daily use.

"Hamilton."

Alec turned at the voice to see an older man approach.

"Ah, Dicky. Wonderful to see you." Hamilton placed a hand on Alec's shoulder. "This is my new boy, Alec."

Dicky ran a hand through his graying but thick hair. He appraised Alec with raised eyebrows. "What a find! Stunning, Hamilton. Will he be open this evening?"

"Not this time. He's here to observe."

"That *is* a shame." The look Dicky gave Alec stirred his interest and made his cock twitch. Dicky ran a hand over his ass which, to Alec's surprise, didn't have him running for the hills at the presumption. "Maybe next time." He gave Alec's ass a gentle squeeze.

"Thank you, sir." Alec thought it seemed like the right response. At that moment, a groan louder than the general hubbub caught his attention. He twisted around to the nearest Chesterfield where he saw the figure of a slender man half-standing, half-kneeling over the large leather sofa. From the angle it was difficult to tell if he was handsome, but his tanned, smooth body boded well. One thing was certain, his enjoyment of being rammed with force from behind by what seemed to be a rather old man was clear from his rock-hard cock. The man fucking him was short, fat, and bald, but his cock looked out of proportion to his body as he pulled out completely before thrusting back in.

"Don't let Worthington's cock scare you, lad," Dicky said with a chuckle. "It only looks so big because he's so small."

"I heard that Dicky," the man said. He glanced over with a grin. "Brendon here thinks my cock is splendid, don't you, Brendon."

"Oh yes, sir. I love your cock."

"Good boy," he said, slapping him hard across the ass cheek. "Tell me how much you want it."

"Fuck me harder, sir, please. I need—oh yes, fuck, yes."

Hamilton squeezed Alec's hand. "Brendon's always very dramatic. I've told them not to encourage him."

At the far end of a matching sofa Alec could see a head bobbing up and down, presumably fucking someone that lay on the floor behind it. To his left in another seating area, a large-built blond sat astride a man in a wide chair. The blond, supported by feet and hands on the arms of the chair, pistoned himself over the cock below. His body was also smooth, cock hard against his belly, face contorted with passion.

"That's my boy, Jules," said Dicky. "He's rather fetching, don't you think?"

"Very," Alec said, swallowing hard. Definitely a turn on, that one. Alec adjusted his painfully hard cock. Watching was going to be more difficult than he'd anticipated given his day so far. His restraint was already at breaking point after a few minutes of the sights, sounds, and smells surrounding him. He'd blow for sure as soon as Hamilton touched him.

"Maybe we can get Alec to fuck Jules for us later, Hamilton, what do you say?"

"Hell yes." Alec clapped his hand over his mouth, his eyes wide. Hamilton and Dicky roared with laughter.

"And I thought you were going to be shy," Hamilton said to Alec and kissed the hand he still held.

"I'm sorry, sir. I have no idea where that came from."

"From your cock, boy," Dicky said as he gave Alec's crotch a firm squeeze. Alec whimpered at the teasing touch.

"Hands off, Dicky," Hamilton warned. "You know the rules."

Dicky raised his hands. "Best behavior." He smiled.

Alec had been so caught up in what was going on around him he hadn't noticed Dicky was naked until he started thumbing his erection. His cock looked nice, considering the guy must have been sixty. A good size, not too veiny. It looked suckable. Alec wondered what it would taste like and licked his lips.

"Your boy seems hungry, Hamilton. Haven't you been feeding him?" His eyes flicked back to Alec. "Do you want to suck it, lad?"

Alec looked at Hamilton, who raised an eyebrow in query. "Do you?"

"I think I do... if I'm allowed, sir."

Hamilton nodded once and Alec dropped to his knees. He looked up at Dicky. He had a kind face, and stroked Alec's cheek as Hamilton had done so often already in their short time together.

"Open up then." Alec opened his mouth and Dicky teased his lips with the head of his cock. Alec smiled and lunged forward to suck in the head. Dicky laughed. "Oh, sweet heavens. Good suction."

"With a little more practice, he's really going to be something special," Hamilton said. He stroked Alec's hair. "Good boy. Don't try to take too much just yet. That's it, just play with the tip."

"How new is new?"

"Would you believe he started yesterday."

"Definitely a natural. Do let me know if you're looking to move him on."

Alec blanked out the words. He didn't want to think about what they meant, he just wanted to concentrate on the job at hand. It took a while but he was rewarded with a mouthful of warm fluid for his efforts, which he swallowed, not wanting to spill any on his clothes. Alec made a mental note to ask Hamilton later whether it had been the right thing to do. He sat back to lick his lips and looked up at Hamilton with a smile.

"Wonderful, Alec. Well done."

"Thank you, sir." Alec looked up at Dicky who was wiping his brow. "And thank you, sir, for allowing me to service you."

"It was *my* pleasure. You've got a good one there, Hamilton."

Alec's heart skipped a beat. Hamilton would be pleased with him. It seemed pretty straightforward to say the things that were expected. Alec had watched enough period dramas with his mother to know how servants addressed their masters and this seemed similar in many ways. He found he kind of liked it. When Hamilton praised him it went straight to his cock and made him feel warm inside. Having the acknowledgement from Dicky was similar—it felt good. Even better was the added bonus of extra attention from Hamilton. Win-win situation. Alec would definitely be looking to suck more cocks.

Hamilton's clipped tone broke into his pleasant thoughts. "Why is Sebastian in the corner?"

Alec looked over to see a small quivering body on its knees, forehead pressed to the floor.

A voice from behind interrupted. "I sent him there until you returned to deal with him." Alec didn't like the man's tone, when he turned to see who the voice belonged to, he didn't like the man either. He was tall, well over six feet and painfully thin. There was a haughtiness to him, and hawk-like features made his face hard and twisted. "I know you don't like your boys to be disciplined by anyone else."

"And tell me, Arland, why does he need to be disciplined?"

"He was being defiant. Refused to submit to me. I had to use Dylan instead."

"Sebastian, heel."

The boy—and he really did look a youngster—scurried over and touched his lips to Hamilton's shoe. "I'm so sorry, Master. I didn't mean to embarrass you."

"Go to your room, Sebastian. I will see to you later."

"Please, Master, I can still be of service."

"Do I have to ask you again?"

"No, Master." The boy kissed Hamilton's shoe again and walked slowly from the room. Even in his despondent mood, he had more of a sensual slink than a walk. It emphasized his slight frame and his killer ass. Alec found himself mesmerized right up to the point he disappeared from view.

"Time you were rid of that one, Hamilton," Arland said. "Always has been a problem."

Alec didn't think Sebastian looked like any kind of a problem. But then, what did Alec know?

"The problem, Arland, is that you insist on using Sebastian when he's not suitable to your needs."

"He's a slave. It's his function to be suitable to all needs. If you didn't spoil him, he would take it as he should, without complaint."

"I will not have this conversation with you again. I think the time has come for us to part company. You will not be welcome here anymore. Please leave."

Arland straightened to an even more imposing height and his features tightened around a heavy scowl. "You're making a mistake, Hamilton."

Alec felt the weight of the threat and leaned instinctively into Hamilton's side. Hamilton didn't falter.

"You can threaten me all you like. My first duty is to the welfare of my boys. I shall make sure you are excluded from a lot of households, should you wish to test my patience any further."

"And I shall second it," Dicky added. "Your needs are better served elsewhere."

"Very well." The man picked up his clothes and threw a wad of money at Hamilton's feet. "For services rendered." He left the room without dressing.

"Good riddance to bad blood," Dicky said. "Your boy did very well to stand up to him, Hamilton. Don't be too hard on him."

Hamilton patted Dicky's shoulder. "Thank you for your support."

Alec looked around the room to see Brendon, Jules and what he presumed to be Dylan being fucked by different men. Brendon also had a cock in his mouth and a third in his hand. The three men who had been in various stages of fucking when Alec arrived appeared around them.

Worthington looked down at Alec. "So this is the new boy?"

"Lovely eyes," another said, stroking his hair.

"How long before he's available?" said the third.

Alec felt like a dog being petted and pawed. But worse than that were the three cocks dangling in his face. He closed his eyes and tried to breathe.

"A little space please, gentlemen. Alec, you may stand, you know."

"Oh, yes. I forgot." He stood up and felt much better.

"Do we get to see him naked?" Worthington said.

"Yes of course. He'll be fucking Jules as soon as he becomes available. Alec strip. You can leave your clothes in the hall."

Alec nodded once and went back to the closet where Hamilton had hung his jacket. He hesitated as he caught sight of Arland slipping into his shoes. He glared briefly at Alec before snatching his jacket and storming out of the door, leaving it to slam behind him. Alec let out a relieved breath; at least he wouldn't have to get on his knees for such a bully. This was it: decision time. He could either strip off and be ogled and groped by these men, watched while he had his second-ever fuck with a complete stranger, or he could grab his jacket and leave. He was surprised to find he was already removing his clothes while he debated what would be best. Damn, it was so easy to take orders from that man. And he wanted to fuck Jules. In front of everyone. Maybe he was a closet exhibitionist. He'd sucked Dicky's cock without being asked. Had wanted to. In the middle of a crowded room. To please Hamilton. Alec was back at Hamilton's feet before he came to the conclusion that's where he wanted to be. He grinned when Hamilton stroked his cheek.

"My beautiful boy," Hamilton said, and Alec knew he was in the right place. His cock was certainly happy, standing to attention for the world to see.

There followed a short conversation about how good Alec looked. He wasn't shy at being naked. He knew he had a good body: not over-defined but well-muscled; slim hips; the slightest ripple of abs; and he was very proud of the oblique definition that gave him a V-shape to showcase his cock. The one aspect in which he differed from the other boys was the light smattering of hair over his chest and his neatly trimmed pubes. His fellow houseboys were all smooth. Dicky rubbed a hand over Alec's chest, pulling at the hair while the men discussed what they preferred. Alec smiled at him. Dicky was a sweetheart. He explained that he'd encouraged Jules to go natural but the boy would have none of it. Alec saw Jules, who must have overheard Dicky, laughing about it as a man with a wave of gray hair fucked him over the arm of the sofa. They chatted to each other as though over cups of coffee.

Alec had heard and forgotten the other two men's names. But the one who had been fucking Dylan behind the sofa was getting hard again as he watched Hamilton stroke Alec's shoulder. The man smiled at Alec and he wondered if he should offer to service him. He looked like an average guy, no real distinguishing features. But he seemed to be important.

"I'm overdressed," Hamilton said. "I'm just going to change. Will you be okay here for a moment?"

"Yes, sir."

"Would you like to service someone while I'm gone?"

"If you'd like me to."

"As you wish. Gentlemen please don't crowd him. It's his first time. And not too deep."

The man who had been growing harder pulled Alec's chin to face him. "Can I jump the line?"

Alec quirked a smile. He knelt down and opened his mouth to take in the head of the man's cock. He was disappointed not to have Hamilton stay to watch but Alec figured if he managed to get off one and be on another by the time Hamilton returned he would be pleased. What he was beginning to realize with this fourth cock was that each was different and needed a little something different to get off. But it wasn't long before he was swallowing down the man's cum. He licked his lips as the cock slipped from his mouth and turned to the next guy in line. He could hear the last one singing his praises as he looked up to register the new man's smile and then opened his mouth and took in cock number five. Not bad for a virgin on his second day at sex school. This time the man pulled out and let the cum spray over his face. He jerked a little at first but opened his mouth to receive it. He got a pat on the head for that one. Someone handed him a towel. He looked up to say *thank you* and found Hamilton smiling down at him.

"Well done, Alec. You're doing very well."

"Thank you. I'm having a nice time."

The men laughed and he moved on to Worthington's cock, which was definitely bigger. By the time he was done, Jules was waiting for him. The men all took a seat around a low central table where Jules sat cross-legged, erection facing the ceiling, and wearing a killer grin. Brendon went to sit on Dicky's lap, impaled on his cock by the look of the way he wriggled over Dicky and leaned back against his chest. Dylan curled up at Worthington's feet.

Alec flushed. Hamilton helped him to stand. "I don't know what they're expecting to see," Alec said. "It's not as if I'm actually any good at it."

Jules laughed but Hamilton stroked his back. "I'll be with you again, just like yesterday," he said so that only Alec could hear. "Remember, you are an extension of my body. I'm the one fucking Jules."

Alec nodded, feeling much better. He could handle that. Hamilton kissed his neck and shoulders, soft hands tracing lines over his body and he trembled. What he really wanted was to bend over and let Hamilton play with his ass. The hunger prickled within him and he leaned in to Hamilton's touch. Hamilton led him over to the table and to his knees.

Alec looked at Jules. He was stunning. All blond and golden. Jules slid to the edge of the table and placed his arms around Alec's neck. "Hey, new kid," he grinned. "Want to kiss a little first?" Back into Alec's comfort zone. He smiled and zoned in. It started out tender, exploratory. Jules tasted of fresh sweat and cum and sex, and Alec felt every touch of their lips shoot straight to his cock. Teeth clashed and tongues tangled. Alec let his hands explore the body in front of him. Hamilton's hand was firm where it rubbed Alec's back. The caress spurred him on and kept him grounded in his need. Jules groaned into Alec's mouth until Alec broke away to slide his lips over Jules's chin and down his neck. He kissed, bit, and nibbled his way south until he lapped the head of Jules's cock.

"Fuck, that's good, new kid. I am loving you already."

Alec chuckled as he teased. He could see Brendon from the corner of his eye, rocking gently over Dicky's cock as the older man's gaze fixed on Alec and he felt his own cock twitch. Definitely an exhibitionist. He wanted to turn Jules into a quivering mess the way Hamilton did with him, in a way these men didn't seem to bother to do. But Alec wasn't here for his own need, he was here to put on a show and a show was what they'd get.

He licked the length of Jules's cock and kneaded his balls with a gentle hand. "Turn over for me."

42

Jules curled over gracefully and planted himself in front of Alec, knees either side of his, and nestled his ass back against Alec's leaking cock. Alec nibbled into the crease of his neck and shoulder, hands dipping over his stomach to stroke Jules's cock. In response, Jules moaned and writhed back against him. Alec's cock skipped over Jules's ass crack and nestled between his thighs to butt against his pucker

Hamilton pulled Alec back for a moment and rolled a condom over his cock. "Are you ready to fuck him for me?" Alec turned his head and kissed Hamilton, keeping his hands on Jules as he moved against him. Hamilton's hands guided Alec's hips and in the next moment tight heat wrapped around him and he groaned. Alec looked down to see Jules moving, fucking himself. Alec hadn't needed lube or a finger, just slipped straight in and it felt incredible. Not as tight as Michael, but then Jules had been screwing for hours. Hamilton whispered in Alec's ear and thrust his hips forward to meet Jules's movements.

Alec spread Jules's ass cheeks so he could see his cock disappearing inside that hot body. "Fuck, that's amazing." He moved a hand to his cock and waited until Jules moved forward. When he pushed back Alec added a finger underneath his cock and Jules bucked his hips.

"Fuck yes, more. I want more." Alec left his finger wriggling as Hamilton thrust Alec's hips faster. He added another finger, felt around for Jules's sweet spot, and relished the extra tightness and his own fingers rubbing the underside of his cock. Jules bucked again as Alec hit gold. Concentrating on massaging that spot took Alec's mind off his own need to come. Jules wasn't doing so well. His body shuddered, his head fell forward, and he started to whimper and plead as his movements became more desperate. Alec used his other hand to stroke over Jules's back and then pulled his head back by his hair. A delicious sound escaped Jules's throat. Alec wanted to catch it with his

43

mouth. He kissed Jules all over his back, and bit, sucked, and licked the sweat from his body. A cry of his own went up as he felt Hamilton's cock slip between his own cheeks and brush over his hole. Alec wanted it, wanted that cock lodged deep inside his body. But Hamilton let go of Alec's hip and batted his cock out of the way to replace it with his thumb. Alec felt it ride over his pucker.

Jules stretched out, arms over his head, forehead pressed against the table, and a slow whine began in his throat.

Hamilton's breath rolled over Alec's neck. "Dicky is going to tell him to come. When he does Alec, you'll feel his body clench around you. Remove your fingers and thrust as hard and fast as you can. When he's finished, you pull out, slip off the condom and come over his back."

Alec nodded, struggling to concentrate as Hamilton swapped the thumb pressing against his pucker for a finger and pushed it in farther. Alec looked up to see Dicky stroking Jules's hair and face. Jules had his cheek pressed against the table and was sucking on Dicky's fingers. Dicky leaned over and kissed his temple. "Come for me, baby."

Jules opened his mouth and cried out. Alec pulled out his fingers, grabbed Jules by the hips, and slammed into him as his ass clenched. Too much sensation. The spiral started in Alec's gut. Jules went limp in his arms. "Now Alec," Hamilton whispered. Alec pulled out, slipped off the condom, and groaned as he spilled over Jules's sated body. Hamilton smoothed his back in what was becoming a familiar way, and Alec leaned over to kiss Jules's sweaty skin as he started to chuckle.

"You got me, new kid," he said. "Fucking fantastic."

"Likewise," Alec whispered in his ear. He peeled himself off Jules's body and stood up. His legs were a little shaky. Hamilton wiped him down with a towel.

He felt arms around his waist and turned into a long sloppy kiss from Jules. "Thanks, babe. See you soon, yeah?"

"Sure," Alec said, not knowing if that was true.

Jules flopped onto Dicky's lap and stretched out on the sofa like a cat. Dicky stroked his stomach lazily. "Nice show, Alec. Jules is rarely so contented."

"I am too," Jules said, flicking Dicky's shoulder. "Don't go giving him an ego."

"Young man, I haven't heard you moan like that in a very long time."

"Then you should see to me more often," Jules complained. "You're always at parties without me lately." He snuggled up against the Dicky's chest. "I miss you, Dicky. You always make me moan."

Dicky looked up at Hamilton and nodded at Alec. "Make sure you don't spoil that boy, or you'll end up with one of these." He patted Jules.

"You love that boy, don't try to deny it," Hamilton said.

"It is true." Dicky chuckled. "Come on, brat, get your clothes on. Hamilton needs to see to his boys before they pop." He slapped Jules's ass as he stood up and Jules winked at Alec.

He'd been so caught up with Jules that he hadn't noticed Brendon and Dylan were both getting fucked again. Hamilton, with an impressive erection of his own, went to Dylan first and started to stroke the boy's hair. Worthington came with a grunt and a thrust and pulled out. Dylan stood up and leaned back against Hamilton, who whispered in his ear. Dylan came hard over Hamilton's hand. He pulled it toward himself and rubbed it into his belly then licked over Hamilton's palm before kneeling to kiss the head of Hamilton's cock.

Hamilton moved on to Brendon who was sat astride one of the men Alec had sucked. He tweaked Brendon's nipples and held his chin. "Come for me, Brendon."

"Ah, Master." Brendon shot over his chest and stomach, hitting Hamilton as well. The man underneath him held him tight and then relaxed. Hamilton helped Brendon to stand and kissed his cheeks, whispering and stroking.

It seemed the party was over as the men started to dress. Dylan and Brendon curled up together on the sofa, hugging and kissing and stroking each other. Hamilton came back to Alec. "You can meet them properly in the morning." He smiled. "How are you feeling?"

Alec grinned back. "I feel great, but you need attention." Alec looked down at Hamilton's erection.

"I'm saving it for you. Let me shower the boys and put them to bed, then I'm all yours."

A trickle of excitement ran over Alec. He picked up a bottle of water from the side table and found a comfy chair. He watched as the men placed large piles of cash on a counter before leaving.

The man he'd sucked after Dicky came over and handed Alec some money. "Take it," he smiled. "It's usual for us to tip boys we're pleased with. You don't need to be offended."

"Thank you, sir." Alec put it on the arm of the chair. He saw that Brendon and Dylan also had money on the floor near them.

Alec looked back at the man. He'd taken out his cock again. "Suck on the end and kiss it for me." Alec sat up and took the semi-hard cock into his mouth. He spent a few minutes sucking and then kissed the end. "Lick the shaft and around the ridge." Alec ran a flat tongue along the underside and pulled back the rest of the foreskin to lick as asked. "You like doing that, don't you?"

"It's what Mr. Hamilton wishes me to do, sir, so yes, I like it."

The man put his cock away and smiled. "I hope to see you soon, Alec. You're very attractive and well behaved. But I want to fuck you next time. Do you think that will be something you'd like?"

"Um, I don't know what Mr. Hamilton wants of me yet, sir. I'm not a houseboy."

"Oh, of course, I remember, silly of me." He handed Alec a business card; Miles Henry, it read. "This is my private number. Call me when you're available. I'll make it worth your while." He handed Alec another wad of cash. "Don't leave it too long. I'd like to fuck you a few times before you're available to everyone else. It can be our secret."

Alec was about to say he wouldn't keep secrets from Hamilton but the man put a finger to his lips to silence him and then left. Alec sighed. There were bound to be a few odd ones.

Worthington came over. "Be careful with him." He moved the money and the card to one side and sat on the arm of the chair. He placed an arm around Alec's shoulder. "Henry will fuck you and forget you. He only comes to parties when there's a new boy. Keep the money. Throw the card away. You're a lovely boy, Alec. You did very well this evening. Very hot show."

"Thank you, sir. I had fun. You've all been lovely to me."

Worthington chuckled. "Dear boy, don't forget we're being lovely to you because we want you to suck our cocks and bend over to be fucked like good little boys."

"I know that, sir, but you don't have to be friendly and kind as well. We'd still have to serve you."

"You mean, Arland. Yes, nasty piece of work that one. He'd have torn a strip off Sebastian if Dicky hadn't caught on to what was happening. Tried to drag the boy into one of the bedrooms. He knows the rules but he chooses to break them. Well, I must be off. Lovely meeting you. I'll probably see you at the office. I'm on the twelfth."

Alec smiled. "I'll look out for you, sir." He kissed Worthington's palm as Worthington stroked his cheek and got another chuckle out of him before he left.

A Whole New World

Hamilton appeared with Sebastian. The poor thing looked as though he'd been crying. A lot. He sat the boy at Alec's feet and ushered Brendon and Dylan out of the room. Alec wasn't sure what to do, so he sat on the floor next to him. "I'm Alec."

"Master, told me."

"Are you okay?"

"No, that horrible man always tries to get me into trouble." His head fell against Alec's shoulder and Alec put an arm around him. His shoulders were warm and he fit perfectly, nestled into Alec's side. Every now and then, a shudder snaked through his body and Alec squeezed him, just a little, until it passed. They sat like that, in silence, until Hamilton came back about fifteen minutes later.

"Lovely picture," Hamilton said, smiling at them. He sat on the sofa and patted his knee. Sebastian sat on his lap and leaned against him. "And you, Alec," he said. "Sit next to me." Alec settled onto the sofa facing Sebastian. "What happened this time?"

"I'm so sorry, Master. I was fucking Worthington when you left, you know he's always gentle with me and Arland was making fun. Afterward Arland grabbed me for a blowjob, which of course I gave him. He was about to come I swear, but he pulled out and said he wanted to fuck me because it wasn't working. I asked him how he wanted me. I promise I didn't fight. But you know he likes to be rough. He said he was going to fuck me so hard I'd feel him for a week. I still got into position for him but he wasn't going to use any lube so I moved away and asked him to use some. He told me I was insolent but I know you don't like them to be rough if you're not here." He paused as another shudder ran through him and Hamilton stroked his back and murmured in his ear until he settled. "You're always with me, Master," Sebastian continued, "when they want it hard, and I was scared he wouldn't stop if it hurt. He dragged me into the hall and slapped me, forced his cock down my throat. I couldn't breathe. He held me there and watched me struggle. I started to cry." His shoulders slumped. "I'm so pathetic."

"Don't be silly, Sebastian." Hamilton brushed his lips lightly over Sebastian's cheek. "I won't have you think of yourself that way."

"I'll take my punishment, Master. I know I'm not as good as your other boys." Sebastian paused again, then seemed to collect himself. "He tried to push me into the bedroom but I wouldn't go. He wanted to beat me but Dicky realized I was missing from the room. He sent Arland to Dylan and told me to wait in the corner for you. Dicky pretended to be angry with me, but I know he was just helping."

The motion of Hamilton's hand over Sebastian's skin was mesmerizing, and so was his focus, every ounce of it directed toward soothing and relaxing the tight ball of nerves huddled on his lap. Alec could see the tension in Sebastian's muscles loosen and melt away. It was fascinating. "And what did Arland do with Dylan?"

"You know Dylan likes it rough. He took him without lube and Dylan let him pin him down with his arms up his back. He even fought back for him." Sebastian stared at his hands where they sat in his lap. "I'm sorry I'm not better."

"Sebastian, I will not punish you for doing the right thing."

"But you sent me away," he said, looking up into Hamilton's face.

Hamilton tweaked the end of his nose and smiled. "I wanted you to rest. I'm sorry if you felt it was because I was angry with you. I sent Arland home. He won't be coming here again."

"Really, Master, you're not disappointed?" The bubbling of hope in Sebastian's voice pulled at Alec's chest.

"No, sweetheart. It was my failing. I shouldn't have left you. Now…" Hamilton's gentle smile broadened into a grin. "I think you deserve something a little special. Alec, come and suck Sebastian's cock. Make him feel better."

Alec smiled. "I'd love to." Sebastian stayed on Hamilton's lap, but stretched out. For a little guy he had a nice size cock, quite thick, even without being fully hard. Alec worshipped that cock with Hamilton's fingers threading through his hair. It felt so right, like this was where he belonged. Hamilton whispered in Sebastian's ear and he shot into Alec's mouth. Sweet compared to the other cum he'd swallowed that night. He didn't want to let go of the cock and Hamilton had to nudge him away.

"I'm going to put Sebastian to bed."

Alec breathed in the silence of the apartment as they left him alone. A far cry from the heated thrust and grunt of an hour before. There was something special hanging in the air, maybe the left over residue of so much sex, so much ecstasy. There was certainly a distinct smell that lingered, but Alec thought it could be the promise of what was still to come—Hamilton's undivided attention for one—and, he was sure, along with it would be a whole host of breath-taking experiences to top everything he'd sampled so far.

When he came back, he held out a hand to Alec and led him through the bedroom to the bathroom. They showered together and Hamilton showed Alec how to use an enema to clean himself out. They kissed and stroked and Hamilton rubbed him down with a towel and led him to bed.

"And now Alec," he said, hot breath rolling over Alec's neck. "Now I'm going to make love to you because you are the most beautiful man I've ever met." Lips were hot and passionate, hands roved, stoking the flames. Alec was soon senseless with need, writhing under Hamilton's attention.

"Take me, please," Alec begged. "I want your cock inside me."

"Do you want to be one of my boys, Alec?"

"Yes, sir, I do."

"You want to serve me?"

"Please, yes please."

Alec felt the head of Hamilton's cock nudge against his well-prepared hole. He wanted to push back against it but Hamilton held him firm and pushed in slowly, and Alec felt the head of Hamilton's cock breach the muscle. He groaned as Hamilton started a slow piston motion, kissing and caressing and filling him completely. How had he lived without this? Lost to the emotion, Alec let his body take over. They loved thoroughly and at Hamilton's command, Alec shot his load. As Alec's senses returned, Hamilton rested gently over his body, breathing heavily. After a few more minutes, Hamilton settled beside him. His smile was radiant and Alec grinned in response. Hamilton wrapped him up in a warm embrace, kissing sleepily around his neck and face.

"Thank you, Alec," Hamilton's whispered words tickled Alec's ear. "You're such a gift." And Alec drifted into a contented sleep.

Alec's legs were shaky by the time he made it to breakfast. Well and truly fucked was the expression he thought of and it brought a smile to his face. Hamilton had fucked him repeatedly through the night and in the shower that morning. He was grateful for the couple of day's preparation. He felt nicely sore and achy without it being painful. He received a wonderfully sexy kiss from Sebastian who seemed

51

much brighter despite the teasing from Dylan and Brendon for his show the night before.

Hamilton handed Alec a glass of juice and explained the ropes. "Friday night we have parties, Saturdays together with occasional clubbing during the evening. Sundays are lazy days before the boys go home."

"Where do you all live?"

Brendon slipped a hand over Alec's shoulder and leaned in to his ear. "We have an apartment about twenty minutes away. You should come stay with us. I have space in my bed."

Alec raised an eyebrow. He wasn't used to such blatant come on's and however good-looking Brendon was, Alec wasn't sure he'd want to be left at Brendon's mercy after seeing him devour so many men the night before. Dark and brooding, with a full pout and deep brown eyes to get lost in ticked all the right boxes, but there was an air of arrogance about Brendon and the way he assumed Alec would enjoy being pawed that made Alec nervous.

"Behave, Brendon," Hamilton said, slapping his bare ass. "Alec has his own place. It's better if it stays that way."

Brendon's hand slipped further down Alec's chest and Alec swallowed deeply. "What do you do, when you're not here?" Alec asked.

"Master pays our rent but we all work, well, part time anyway." Brendon's hand moved on to stroking Alec's cock and he was having trouble concentrating on the conversation. "But we make sure we're free for our weekend bonding sessions." Brendon leaned in to Alec's ear. "I could do with a bonding session right now, Alec, what do you think?"

Was he supposed to be turned on by Brendon's suggestion? Whether he was or not, Alec's traitor cock had its own ideas. Alec looked at his master.

Hamilton grinned and shook his head. "Brendon is particularly hungry over the weekends. He pretends he doesn't get any sex during the week, but I know very well he's rarely out of Dylan's ass Monday through Thursday."

"Exactly." Brendon was practically purring as Hamilton ran a hand between his butt cheeks. "And on weekends I like to have my ass thoroughly plundered to get me through the rest of the week. Dylan prefers to fuck Sebastian."

"And who does Sebastian fuck?" Alec asked, looking at the shy man at the end of the table and trying to think of anything other than asses and the plundering thereof.

"Whoever I'm told to." There was a hint of sadness in his voice but he looked up and smiled at Alec. His sandy hair was fairer than Hamilton's and longer, falling across pale green eyes that looked distant. His light frame and baby face gave him a boyish look and his body was completely smooth. Alec noted a very nice erection growing as he glanced into Sebastian's lap. "Are you going to fuck me today, Alec? I'd like that."

"I was first," Brendon said, disengaging his grip on Alec and throwing a tea towel at Sebastian. "You didn't see the show he put on with Jules last night. I want some of that, right now."

They all jumped when Hamilton thumped the table. "*I'm* the Master in this house, or have you all forgotten?"

Brendon, Dylan, and Sebastian fell to the floor before Hamilton's feet. There was some definite elbowing going on for prime position but in the end, Sebastian settled back a little to let the other boys nearer. Alec wanted to pull Brendon and Dylan out of the way so that Sebastian could get a look in.

"Alec will fuck you all at some point, but right now, he needs to finish his breakfast."

"May I serve his food, Master?" Sebastian asked, his forehead still pressed to the floor.

"I think that would be a wonderful idea, Sebastian. Off you go. Brendon, I want to see you in your room."

"Master." Brendon disappeared.

Hamilton stroked Dylan's back with the tips of his fingers and he gave a delicious shudder. "Yes, I think Alec will fuck you first, Dylan. You've been very well behaved this weekend."

"Thank you, Master. I try to be good for you." Dylan was the biggest of the three boys. About five-nine and nicely muscled, he looked as though he spent a lot of time in the gym. His angular face was very handsome, his skin pale, contrasting the dark brown hair and hazel eyes. Alec wanted to fuck him. Wanted to taste and tease the hard, muscled ass that was staring at him.

"Why don't you suck Alec's cock while he's having his breakfast? I'll be back in a little while."

Alec had trouble with his cereal. It was very distracting to have Dylan between his legs under the table alternating between sucking his cock and balls. "Is Hamilton fucking Brendon?" Alec asked Sebastian, trying not to sound jealous.

"No. Well, he might afterward, but I think he's probably punishing him for being pushy."

"Yeah," Dylan chuckled, taking a minute's break, "he's always pushy. Usually pushing something up my ass. I'd fuck him if he ever gave me the chance."

"I like that you fuck me," Sebastian said, dipping his head under the table. "Otherwise I'd be on my own during the week. Brendon never bothers with me."

"That's because you're Master's pet."

"I am *not*." Sebastian sat down with a humph and folded his arms over his chest like a spoiled child. He looked so endearing, Alec wanted to pat his head and coax a smile out of him.

Dylan took up sucking Alec's cock again and Alec let everything wash over him. When Brendon came back, his ass was bright red and his cock hard and wet. Hamilton looked amused at the sight of Dylan under the table.

"Ah, very good. We shall take this through to the living room. Alec, you will fuck Dylan. And Sebastian, you will fuck Brendon."

"But, Master," Brendon said, falling to Hamilton's feet.

"Do I need to remove you again, Brendon?"

"No, Master."

"Good. Sebastian will be the only one to fuck you for the rest of the day. I suggest you treat him well. If, and I mean *if* you behave, Alec will fuck you tomorrow."

"Thank you, Master."

By Sunday afternoon, Alec had fucked all the boys several times and they had watched as Hamilton fucked him—a lot. Definitely an exhibitionist. He really didn't want to go home.

Once the boys had left, Alec went to get his clothes. He hadn't needed them the whole weekend and it felt strange to think about dressing. His ass was more on the sore side of pleasantly achy now, but Alec still hadn't had enough. He certainly didn't want to go home to an empty flat where he'd end up jerking off to the memories of real bodies pressed against him.

"Alec," Hamilton said, coming up behind him in the hall. "You don't have to go yet."

"If I don't go now, I won't want to."

"Stay tonight," he said, taking hold of Alec's hand. "I'd like an evening with just the two of us. There are some things I'd like to discuss with you."

Like how Alec wouldn't usually be here on a weekend, because he was just an office boy. It cut through him, made him ache in the wrong ways. Hamilton led him back through to the living room and they stood awkwardly.

"I know you're happy to be my office boy. I wondered if after this weekend you'd like to be something of a houseboy too."

"For you?" *Fucking hell's bells. What a result.*

"Just for me. Alec, I've told you I won't give you to anyone else to fuck. Not even the boys. But I think we… the sex has been good for you… with me, hasn't it?"

"Oh, it's been a revelation," Alec agreed. "Really, sir, incredibly good sex."

Hamilton slipped his arms around Alec's waist. Their cocks nestled together despite the few inches difference in height. Alec had long legs that brought their hips to the same level. "Call me Rick, when we're here alone, Alec. You're not my slave and we aren't at work."

"I'd like very much to be with you at weekends… Rick." He spoke shyly, but pulled Hamilton in for a kiss. There was some kind of open permission in the air for Alec to follow his own needs and he let his hands stray over Hamilton's body.

"I thought perhaps you might want to be here during the week sometimes too." Hamilton let his head fall back so that Alec had better access to kiss over his neck and shoulders. "Damn I'm not being very clear." He gasped as Alec nipped at the skin along the curve of his neck. "I love that you're just mine, Alec. I've never had that before and I want you to be here when I get home. I love having you in my bed. I don't want to rush you but…"

All Alec could hear were the words 'you're just mine.' *I'm his. His alone.* Alec started to tremble. It was more than he could have wished for.

"Are you okay? You don't have to decide now."

He fell at Hamilton's feet. It seemed the natural thing to do. "I love being yours," he said. He kissed Hamilton's toes and ankles before making his way up to wrap his arms around Hamilton's waist. "I want to be just yours, always." Before Hamilton could answer Alec kissed his cock, then sucked it a little, then kissed it again as it started to grow against his lips. He sucked it down. It wasn't the best blowjob but it was sloppy and wet enough that they didn't have to go for lube when Hamilton flipped Alec over and started fucking him. It was a sweet orgasm of longing and belonging. "Thank you, Master," Alec said, as he kissed the end of Hamilton's nose.

"Do you understand what that title means, Alec?"

Alec snuggled closer. "I feel so safe in your arms. You make the decisions that I can't make for myself and you know what I need. This feels so right."

"Thank you, sweetheart. I'm honored and if I'm honest relieved to take you as my boy. But we'll take it slow. You're a natural but there are things we should discuss, boundaries to make sure we are both happy."

"I trust you, Rick, to show me." Sweet sloppy kisses followed that led into a slow sensual dance of lovemaking.

Fathers and Sons

The weeks disappeared in a haze of cocks and fucking. Alec wondered what on earth he used to do with his time before Hamilton and his crazy world exploded into his life. He was sure he'd had more sex in those few weeks than some people in regular relationships had in a year. But he loved every damn minute of it.

Worthington turned up a few times to have Alec suck him off. On each occasion he stroked Alec's cheek and then asked if he was ready to be fucked yet. He'd then remind Alex not to get caught up with Henry, the guy from the party who had given Alec a business card and told him to call. Alec had already had the pleasure of his company once since the party. Miles Henry had made a point of visiting Alec on a day when Hamilton was out of the office and invited him out for something to eat. Alec managed to get a call through to Hamilton for advice which consisted of being extra vigilant and remaining in control. Hamilton also suggested staying in public places, which didn't fill Alec with confidence, but he went to lunch determined to prove he could handle the situation. When Alec declined Henry's request to visit a hotel, he was not impressed. He did take up the offer of a blowjob in the taxi, however, and he was rough. Alec spent most of the time gagging, eyes streaming as Henry forced his cock as far in as it would go. But he did tip Alec two hundred pounds and made it clear the next time he would get fucked. It reinforced Alec's decision not to accept an invitation from Henry again unless Hamilton requested it of him. Alec gave the tip to the cabbie and smiled for the rest of the afternoon remembering the look on the guy's face as he handed over the money and told him to keep the change.

Alec looked out of the window in Hamilton's office, at the streets below. He felt far removed from the daily lives of those people scurrying around. The eight floors between him and the street may as well have been a thousand.

Hamilton stood behind him and rested his chin on Alec's shoulder. "What are you thinking about?"

"How much my world has changed." Alec turned to kiss Hamilton's cheek.

"It's about to change a little more. I would have liked to talk to you about this at home but it's a short-notice thing."

Alec turned to put his arms around Hamilton and sighed contentedly as Hamilton pulled him close. "I'll do whatever you need me to do, you know that." Things had progressed between them. Alec was comfortable in Hamilton's embrace, even more so in his bed, but there as an unspoken trust that allowed Alec to follow Hamilton's direction knowing he was being well guided. It took much of the stress out of his personal life and Alec regularly reviewed how lucky he was to have stumbled on such an ideal situation—as much sex as he wanted with multiple partners and yet he still had someone special.

"We have a lunch date." Hamilton said, seeming a little more pleased by Alec's response. "It's a meeting really. I wasn't going to take you but Worthington has asked for you personally."

"He likes my blowjobs."

"He wants your ass. Anyway, it seems he's been advertising your services and everyone wants to meet Hamilton's new boy. I could thump him, really."

"I'm sure he means well."

"Actually, he does. It will be a good opportunity for you to meet some important clients. I'm taking three other boys along but you'll be busy because they don't know you."

"And I just suck cock when I'm asked?"

"It's all code at these things. They will start a conversation with you about business. If they decide they want to work with you they'll suggest you retire to discuss the details."

"And that's when they want me naked."

"They will expect you to service them, yes. You don't need to undress and they'll just unzip and offer their cock. For goodness sake, don't get cum on their suits or yours."

"Do you think I'm good enough to be able to do this, Rick?"

Hamilton squeezed him and the kiss on his neck sent shivers right through his body. "You are perfect, Alec. I just wanted to keep you to myself a little longer."

"They'll fuck me?"

"Heaven's no, but they will pick you rather than me offering your service. You're going to be very popular."

Alec nestled into the crook of Hamilton's neck. "I thought you liked seeing me suck cock for you."

"I do, I can't explain why. It's not the same as the other boys. But I won't see you, you'll be alone with them and I don't like the idea of it. I don't trust all of them and neither should you. Anyway, we should be leaving."

"Rick, if you need to let these guys fuck me—"

Hamilton's grip on Alec's waist tightened. "Absolutely not. Your ass is mine, do you understand?"

Alec grinned. "Yes, sir. I understand perfectly."

It was a very exclusive hotel and there were easily forty people in attendance, including a smattering of women. Hamilton kissed Alec on the cheek, told him to spit not swallow before introducing him to a middle-aged gentleman with dyed brown hair and rounded shoulders. The man wasn't bad looking, but he didn't exactly ignite any sparks. Alec watched as Michael, Glen, and Mehmet, the other office boys on duty, started to mingle.

"Peter Worthington tells me your portfolio performed very well last quarter." Alec turned his attention to the client. Interesting, as far as Alec was aware, Worthington knew nothing of Alec's job performance.

Alec smiled. "My clients have been very happy. Is there something in particular I can help you with?"

The man gave Alec the once over and smiled. "I think we should retire to discuss this further, Alexander," the man said. He hadn't given his name, so Alec hadn't asked for it.

"Certainly, sir. Do lead the way."

Alec followed to a row of discreet booths at one end of the hall that could easily have been for voting. Inside was a small counter, a chair, and a floor cushion. A fluffy towel and a stainless steel bowl with a cloth to hide the contents sat on the counter. *Spit, not swallow* made sense now. The opening side faced the wall to keep the happenings discreet, if not completely private.

Alec stepped in first and turned to face his client.

"You can sit if you like, I prefer to stand." The man unzipped his pants and flopped out his flaccid cock. "You *do* service?" he asked, as Alec looked at it.

"Absolutely, sir." Alec sat on the chair and looked up with a smile. "I was just waiting for you to get comfortable."

The man stepped forward and pushed his cock against Alec's lips. Alec opened to suck it in, making sure he didn't close his eyes. He didn't want to give the impression he didn't want this. This man had to leave knowing Alec was willing to serve his needs. But more than that, this man had to think he was important enough to warrant all of Alec's attention and be impressed enough to tell Hamilton how great Alec was. With Hamilton in the back of his mind, Alec set to work worshipping the man and the cock in front of him.

It wasn't long before muffled noises started to seep in from the cubicles on either side. Alec recognized Michael's voice to the right. From the grunting and slight vibration of the wall, Alec figured Michael wasn't sucking cock. The extra stimulation tipped Alec's guy over the edge. Alec milked his cock and carefully spat the contents into the bowl before cleaning them both up.

"Thank you, Alexander. I look forward to working with you." Alec stood to shake his hand and the guy groped Alec's ass. "I'm sure you have a lot more to offer."

"It will be my pleasure, sir." Though what kind of investment service the client required and whether Alec could deal with it, he still had no clue.

"May I see?"

Alec puzzled for a moment. "I'm sorry, what would you like to see?"

The man pulled at Alec's pants and dropped them to the floor. He fondled Alec's cock and watched it harden. "Lean over the counter." Alec did as he was told. At least the guy wasn't hard so there would be no surprise penetration. Hands spread his ass cheeks and a finger probed his ass. "Are you fucked often?"

"I have a partner, sir, but I'm not fucked as part of my role with the company."

"Why ever not?"

"I'm still in training. This is my first meeting."

The man tapped his ass cheek. "Buckle up, Alexander. I'm more than happy to work with you without you handing over fucking rights." The guy smiled. "Thank you for letting me have a poke around. Oral service is more than enough to seal this particular deal."

He patted Alec on the shoulder as Alec tucked himself back in. "Thank you, sir. I'm still getting used to what's expected of me."

"A word to the wise, when the next guy asks you to drop your pants, say no."

"Why is that?"

"As soon as you bend over that counter you're giving permission to be fucked and that's not why you're here. You're lucky I have a conscience. On a different day I would have just taken you."

Alec flushed scarlet. "I didn't realize. Thank you for explaining."

"You're welcome, lad. Let me introduce you to a friend of mine. You will need to be very firm with him, but he's a good contact."

Alec was led from the booth and introduced to another man, older than the first, heavier but handsome. His blue eyes sparkled as he raked over Alec's body. Within a few minutes, Alec was back in the booth with the man's cock in his mouth.

It continued like that, Alec didn't make it more than a few feet away from the booth the entire time he was there. His reward was a brilliant smile from Hamilton every time he emerged with an arm around his shoulder and a firm handshake from his client. A much easier way to do business, Alec decided, than endless meetings and disagreements over the small print.

Weekends were boy time, but the one or two weeknights Alec went to Hamilton's were his alone. His favorite time, and he hoped Hamilton's too. Chloe Fleming and Tom Parsons congratulated him on his efforts toward what they figured was an upcoming promotion. In private Chloe teased Alec about him finally being able to stop with the puppy eyes at Hamilton. Alec hadn't realized how obvious he must have been before. It was embarrassing to a point and at the same time a relief to know he was managing to be more discreet.

He was just finishing some paperwork when Hamilton called him into his office. Alec was surprised to see three men with him. Well, two men; the third could easily be a teenager.

"Alec, I'd like you to service these gentlemen for me. Please lock the door and remove your clothes."

Alec stripped off immediately and took up the position on his knees by the desk. The first man came to stand in front of him and dropped his pants. He was probably in his late sixties, slightly overweight and very hairy. Alec looked up at him.

"Well get on with it, boy. I don't have all day."

Alec pulled the front of the man's boxers down and found the smallest cock he'd ever seen. It was starting to show signs of life as he took it in his mouth. He was able to suck it in to the root without it choking him but the hairs tickled his nose and caught in his teeth. He persevered, pleased he could at least get a good suckling action. The man pulled out and shot over his face. "Lick it clean," he said in an impatient tone. "I don't want to be sticky all afternoon."

So this was the reality. Grumpy old men who didn't really like you, but you still had to suck, bow, and scrape. He pushed the thought from his mind and sucked the cock to make sure it was clean before he tucked it away for the man. "Thank you, sir." Alec bowed his head.

"The boy needs practice," Grumpy told Hamilton. "It's no good having them for show. They have to be able to perform."

"Alec is still in training, sir."

Fuck, Hamilton was calling *him* sir. Oh, god and Alec had given him a crap blowjob. *Fuckity fuck*. Hamilton came over and stroked Alec's neck.

"Well hurry up with it," Grumpy said. "You have the means at your disposal to ensure it happens quickly. Make sure he's ready when I'm here again." Grumpy made his way back to his seat and huffed as he sat heavily.

Hamilton bowed his head just a little and sat down at the desk. Interesting there had been no introductions. But then Alec hadn't known the names of most of the men he'd sucked at the lunch either. The young man stood up next. As he stood before Alec, it was obvious he was older than first impressions had led him to believe, but probably not more than twenty. He was very feminine with a slight build, a fluff of dark longish hair, and delicate features. His eyes were so brown they looked almost black.

He walked around Alec a few times trailing fingers around his shoulders then grabbed Alec's hair and yanked his head back. "Why doesn't he fuck? I want to—"

Hamilton jumped up had slapped the boy's hand away. "You would do well to learn some manners from your father, young man. Alec is not a dog for you to kick when you need entertaining."

Alec automatically put his forehead to the floor to keep out of the way of the fire about to erupt.

"I do apologize, Mr. Hamilton," the young man said. "I'm still finding my feet with these things."

"Then learn from the beginning that you should treat these men with the respect they deserve."

"Quite right too." The last man's voice was deep and authoritative. Obviously the head honcho, even over the little hairy one. "I'm appalled at your behavior, Jasper. What on earth were you thinking?"

"Forgive me, father. It wasn't my intention to displease you."

Alec chanced a look in the direction of the commanding voice. The man, in his fifties but well-built and still handsome, came to stand next to Alec and his son, Jasper. "I think some compensation is in order for the boy. Alec, you may stand." Alec stood to face him. Poor Jasper was trembling. "What would you like, Alec?"

"He didn't hurt me, sir. There's no need for me to be given anything."

"I didn't ask if you were hurt. I asked what you wanted."

Damn, he'd fucked up again. He fought the urge to kneel and apologize. Instead, he hung his head. "I'm very sorry, sir. I don't know what to say."

The man stood behind Alec and ran a hand over his ass. Fingers slipped between his butt cheeks and Alec leaned forward slightly to give better access. The man probed his hole with a finger, pushing into him. Would Hamilton be able to say no to these men if they decided to fuck him? "He doesn't feel particularly tight, Hamilton. Is there a reason he's not available?"

"No, sir. It's just that he hasn't finished his training." There was a tension in Hamilton's tone Alec hadn't heard before and in some small way, Alec appreciated it.

"It's such a shame he doesn't fuck. I'd have given him Jasper's ass as recompense."

Jasper gasped, grabbing his father's arm. "Please father, no. You can't."

"He fucks other men," Hamilton said. "He just isn't available to be fucked."

"Splendid. Jasper, you will remove your clothes and bend over the desk."

"Father, please don't so this."

Freaky families. Alec certainly had no intention of taking the boy against his will. He'd rather be sacked and lose Hamilton than get into that crap.

"Jasper, I won't tell you again. You will learn some manners. You're going to have to suck poor Alec back to strength. Your whingeing has made him wilt."

Jasper started to remove his clothes.

"Alec," the father said. "Lean over the desk. I want to take a better look at your pucker."

That, he could do. Damn, the old man could fuck him if he wanted, rather than Alec have to fuck his kid. He took up his position, hands on the edge of the desk, and leaned over. "Hamilton, pass me the lube and hold the boy's cheeks apart."

Hamilton stroked Alec's back as he always did to calm and reassure him and then held his cheeks open. A slicked up finger pushed straight inside. Alec knew he wouldn't be tight. Hamilton had spent most of the night fucking him senseless and taken him during the morning tea break. "This boy is well used," the father announced, adding another finger and wriggling around. Hamilton's rule of one finger, already broken. *Here comes the cock, obviously.*

Alec jumped as a wet mouth suctioned itself around his cock. He looked down to see Jasper knelt beneath him. *Well fuck me; he does what daddy tells him.*

"Hamilton."

"Sir, he has already been fucked twice today and because of that he is not available for use. I'm very careful not to over-use the boys in their first few weeks. If they get sore, it can make them nervous. Slow, steady increase brings the best results."

"Now that I can agree with. Very well. Fucked by whom?"

"Me, sir."

"Twice? It's barely lunchtime."

Grumpy huffed again and fidgeted in his seat. "Perhaps you should ensure his mouth is as well used in future."

"Alec stayed at the apartment last night."

The man chuckled, as though he knew that meant something in particular. He removed his fingers. "Damn fine ass. Let's hope he does a better job at sucking my cock after he's fucked Jasper or I'll be taking it and he'll just have to use a cushion."

Alec made a mental note—*give killer blowjob or risk fucking.* Jasper was doing very well on his cock. It certainly wasn't the boy's first time at that. Alec was already rock hard. Now for the bigger dilemma.

"Jasper, come out from under there."

The boy crawled out and Hamilton pulled Alec to stand. He squeezed his arm and gave a strained smile in support.

"What do you say, Jasper?"

Alec met Jasper's eyes. They sparkled with mischief. Obviously, not distraught after all. "Please, Alec," he said. "Forgive me for being disrespectful. I'd like to offer you my ass as a way to apologize."

"Um, I don't—"

"But I want you to," Jasper said, brushing a firm hand over Alec's thigh, "I really do, Alec. If for no other reason, do it because I'm asking so nicely." Jasper's body language had transformed from pleading son to sensual with a hungry, predatory gaze that scrambled Alec's thoughts.

"Oh, okay then," Alec managed to say.

Jasper took a step closer and ran a hand up Alec's chest making him shiver. He leaned in to whisper, "I'm going to enjoy this, sweetie. Don't you worry about a thing." He caught Alec off guard by launching into a full-blown makeout session, his cock battling with Alec's as he curled around his body.

His father laughed. "That's my boy." Alec was vaguely aware of Grumpy making a comment that brought a further chuckle.

Things got considerably weirder from then on. Jasper had a well-used hole all of his own. He didn't need any prep—just a squidge of lube and Alec was balls deep. It took him a while to catch up as Jasper frantically fucked himself on Alec's cock. What felt really strange was the way Jasper' father stood behind him, as Hamilton often did, and with his hands on Alec's hips, fully clothed, he ground against Alec's butt to control his thrusts. He didn't once lay a hand on Jasper. He nibbled and sucked Alec's ears and neck, reached up to tweak his nipples. After a while, he fumbled and freed his cock and Alec felt it riding his crack. Once or twice, it slipped between his cheeks and rubbed over his hole, catching slightly as it did. Alec was convinced the old man would end up fucking him, and without a condom to boot. But he soon pushed it lower and started to frot Alec's thighs instead. As the three of them spiraled further into the heat of it, hands wandered. Jasper reached back to grab his father's hand and pulled it to his hip. Alec realized he was just a tool for what was really going on.

The cock bobbed across Alec's balls and slipped up between his ass cheeks again. "I want you boy," the man whispered in his ear. "Your ass is mine and one day I'll take it."

Alec was about to respond but Jasper beat him to it. "Yes, I want you to take me. All of me. I love you. I want to be yours, always."

Fucking hell's bells. Alec tried to ignore the mental images Jasper's pleading threw at him. An eerie silence had fallen over the rest of the office outside of the slap and groan of the sex. Alec looked over at Grumpy, who was staring hard at a point on the floor a few feet in front of him. Hamilton was making a valiant effort of staring out of the window. The head of the father's cock pressed against Alec's hole, pushing just a little, and bringing his attention firmly back to the action. If the guy kept teasing, Alec would end up putting the damn thing in himself, it was torture, but the old man batted it down again.

"Finish him, while he finishes me, Jasper. Alec found himself spun around and pushed to his knees. The offending cock pushed into his mouth and a very clever tongue licked over his asshole. Alec got to work on the killer blowjob. Not that it made much difference—he felt the man had fucked him anyway. The guy spilled in seconds with a cry. "Come, boy," he gasped. And it seemed Alec and Jasper came at the command. "Hamilton you will fuck this boy right now, even if only for a few strokes. I want to see something up his ass."

Alec was dragged to his feet, pushed over the desk, and rammed with Hamilton's cock. *No lube, fuck.* After coming just minutes before, it was uncomfortable and Alec fought back the urge to wriggle away. At least there was a bit of spit left over and a bit of slick from the fingering. Hamilton wasn't gentle. He'd never been so rough and Alec wondered what he'd done wrong, until the soft hand ran over his back and he relaxed into it.

When Hamilton finally let Alec go, he found himself wrapped up in Jasper's arms. "You're so delicious, Alec. Tell me you'll fuck me again soon, promise me."

"You know where I am." Alec rubbed the boy's back as Jasper kissed him.

"Mm, you're a really good fuck." Jasper reached in to nibble Alec's ear. "And I certainly want to fuck you, very soon," he whispered as he stroked Alec's ass cheeks and ran fingers inside the cleft "Tell me, you want me to fuck you, Alec."

"I fuck who I'm told, Jasper. I don't get to choose."

"But if you could, you'd want me to, wouldn't you?"

Jasper was crushed so tightly to Alec's body, he couldn't think straight. He'd be hard and needing to bend him over again if Jasper didn't let go. "I'd want you, Jasper, if I could choose."

"You are such a good boy, Alec, but an awful liar." Jasper winked and kissed him on the lips before sloping off to get dressed.

"Hamilton, I believe it's time for lunch. Your boy has made me hungry." Jasper's father smiled at Alec. "You were splendid, young man. I'll look forward to the next time we meet."

"Thank you, sir."

Fully dressed and primped, the three left the office. Once the door closed behind them, Hamilton pulled Alec into a hug. "I'm sorry Alec. Did Wessex fuck you?"

So, that was his name. "Almost. His cock started to open me up a couple of times but he just pushed it out of the way."

"I was rough to make sure he wouldn't change his mind and fuck you himself."

"It's fine really. He was so close to me, so intimate, he may as well have just done it."

"It's sad really, the way they love each other. Jasper is desperate for Wessex to fuck him, but the old man refuses. Won't let Jasper touch his cock either. Tragic. They must really like you to trust you the way they did. They guard their privacy closely. It's a great respect they've shown you today. Remember it. I've never seen them lose it like that even in my company."

"If they love each other so much, would it really be so bad for them to have sex?"

"Wessex feels it would weaken his reputation. He's very influential. You'll meet a lot of men who bully their sons, make them do questionable things. I have my money on a few that touch more than they should with boys that wished they wouldn't, but Wessex refuses to give in to Jasper. The boy gets everything else he wants, though Wessex can be a little hard on him sometimes in company."

"Like today?"

"No," Hamilton chuckled. "Jasper played us all very well today and got exactly what he wanted."

"Hmm, I wonder if he'll give lessons on that."

"Is there something you want, Alec? Tell me, and it's yours."

"Just you," Alec said, reaching in for another kiss.

Hamilton slapped his bare ass and smiled. "Get dressed. I have a lunch appointment and I need to think."

Crossing Lines

It was definitely Friday. As per the usual Friday morning discussion, Chloe was detailing the latest information regarding her collection of married men. She also had breaking news about a real-ish boyfriend (which meant the guy must be single and had fucked her more than twice) and the list of Tom's excuses as to why Emma, his girlfriend of three months, was unable to see him for the second weekend in a row. Friday mornings were always a drag in the office. And knowing what lay ahead later at Hamilton's only made the day seem to go slower. Alec was getting used to boy time and all he could think about was the party planned for the evening. He would be joining the boys in the pool, but only to suck cock.

Chloe broke him from his reverie. "What are you doing this weekend, Alec? You've been very shady about your weekends lately."

"Have I? You know my life is boring. I prefer hearing what you get up to."

"I suppose you're up all hours with Hamilton."

Fuck, she couldn't know, she just couldn't. "How do you mean?"

"All the extra hours you're doing at work. I bet he has you working all weekend."

Alec breathed again. His palms felt sweaty. "Ha, yeah that's true. I don't seem to have much time to myself. It's all worth it in the end."

"Have you met his girlfriend?"

"No, he never mentions her."

"Heart of stone that one," she said. "He's still sexy as hell mind you, the icy exterior just works for him. I'd fuck him in a heartbeat and I bet you would too, given half the chance."

"Given half the chance." Alec grinned.

"You shouldn't talk about the boss like that, either of you," Tom said, looking over his cubicle. "Not here anyway, he might hear you."

"True," Chloe stood up to look around. "All boss fuck-stories should be relegated to lunchtime gossip. Not that Licky Lou here..." she dipped her head at Alec, "ever comes to lunch anymore."

"You what?"

"You're always licking Hamilton's ass now. I thought it was getting better, but all that 'yes, sir, no, sir, anything you need Mr. Hamilton, sir' is really getting on my tits. Don't forget your friends, Alec."

"And you're such a *great* friend Chloe." Alec stomped away from her, his face flushed. He could hear Tom giving her a dressing down but it was too late. It hurt. He made his way through to the stairwell and sat on the top step, his favorite place when he needed to think. Chloe saw everything, but if she was that pissed at him, it probably meant others had noticed too. If rumours started to fly around that Alec was crushing on the boss it would mean trouble. Alec rested his head in his hands. Was he really that obvious? He'd have to tone it down a bit outside of Hamilton's office.

Alec jumped as the door opened. Tom gave him one of those it'll-be-okay-sport smiles and patted his shoulder. "Speak of the devil, Hamilton is looking for you."

"Yeah well, he'll have to wait. I've got a life too."

"Don't let Chloe's jealousy screw up your chance at promotion, Alec. She's bitter that she's not the one running around after the boss-man. And we all know why she isn't. Shit, the whole building would have heard some half-cocked story about how they fuck every lunchtime over his desk and he calls her in to the office every time he fancies a blowjob."

Alec chuckled. "Have you been spying on me, Tom?"

"Like it would happen. You are the single most straight-laced guy I have ever met and I'd be surprised if Hamilton was even capable of an erection. The man is cold. Don't stress about it. Nobody thinks you're fucking the boss, or that you want to."

"You know I *do* want to though, right?"

"Sure," he grinned. "So does seventy per cent of the building. He stops traffic in the corridors the way he waltzes through this place. I've never seen a man so confident. It's sickening really."

It was one of the things Alec loved about Hamilton, the backbone of steel that left everyone in awe. But Alec knew far more about the man inside the suit, right down to the birthmark an inch to the left of his cock, and the way his lips parted when he came. The thought was enough to brighten Alec's mood. Alec patted the step next to him and Tom sat down. "So you think Emma's cheating on you?"

"Without a doubt. But I wouldn't give Chloe the satisfaction of owning up to it. Good guys always finish last, right?"

"Not all the time. We get our breaks eventually. Do you mind her fucking around?"

"It's not that. I do in a way, but it's the lying that kills. Why can't she just end it if she doesn't want me anymore, rather than leaving me hanging?"

"Perhaps she does still want you."

"Then why can't she tell me she needs something else? If I'm not good enough in bed, or she likes variety, she should be honest."

"Would you tell her she wasn't any good in bed?"

Tom sighed. "Fair point. Love sucks."

Alec put his arm around Tom's shoulder and leaned against him. "You're a good guy, Tom. You'll find the right girl."

Tom sighed and stared at his shoes. "Now if you were a girl, I think we'd be ideally suited."

Alec laughed and pulled Tom in for a proper hug, kissing him on the forehead. "When you start finding my ass sexy, you let me know, sweetheart."

"Your ass is great—it's the lack of boobs and the presence of dangly bits that's the problem. I'm not really one for stubble either."

"You are priceless."

"I've kissed guys before, Alec. I'm not as wet as Chloe makes me out to be."

"Have you now? Anyone I know?"

"No, mostly in uni. I think I wanted to be gay at one point, but it didn't work out for me." He gave a wry chuckle. "I could only keep it up if there was a chick in the bed with us."

"You've fucked with guys?"

"Just a lot of making out and groping. A guy gave me a blowjob once—it was cool."

"Fuck me, you're a dark horse."

"Yeah, I reckon you are too."

The door banged open and they both jumped. "I'm sorry to interrupt your male bonding session but I have things to do. Parsons, when I sent you to find Alec I didn't expect you to join him for a cuddling session."

Tom nearly fell down the stairs trying to extricate himself from Alec's arms. "I'm sorry Mr. Hamilton. I'll, uh… leave you to it."

Alec didn't turn around. He could feel Hamilton's anger rising off him in waves. So much for the unflustered-man-of-steel image. "Why are you still sat there?"

Alec rubbed his face and sighed. He wanted to explain his concerns regarding what Chloe had blurted out, but now wasn't the time. For the moment, he'd better do some serious ass-kissing. The thought made him smile. He would love to run his tongue over Hamilton's pucker and make him squirm.

"Alec!"

"Sorry, sir. I'm…" Alec turned to look at Hamilton and faltered. He was turning a funny shade of pink. "Shit, I really am sorry, sir."

"*Get* to my office, this instant."

It was more a scrabble of arms and legs than a graceful exit on Alec's part. Hamilton didn't follow straight away, which was probably for the best. Alec would look like he was being led to his execution otherwise. He ignored Chloe and Tom and headed straight for the office. He closed the door behind him and stood for ten minutes before Hamilton returned. On entering the office he locked the door behind him. His usual cool exterior was back in place but it gave Alec no cause to relax.

"I'm sure I don't have to tell you how disappointed I am. Remove your clothes and take up position over the desk."

Alec moved as fast as he could but it still felt too long under Hamilton's watchful gaze. His body trembled as he gripped the edge of the desk and presented his ass.

Hamilton's fingertips ran over Alec's back. He shuddered and his flesh broke out in goose bumps. "I'm sure there is a good explanation for your behavior, but I don't want to hear it. You are to respond to my requests immediately, do you understand?"

"Yes, sir."

"When you do not perform as expected, my job is to punish you."

Alec couldn't help it, his ass clenched at the memory of the spanking he'd received over this very desk on his first day. He noted with interest that his cock perked up at the same thought. The measured trail of fingernails over Alec's skin left a slow, burning buzz in their wake.

"Normally, I would wait until we were at home to carry out your punishment. Obvious reasons of sound control."

Sound control?

"However, you're scheduled for service this evening and it wouldn't look good to advertise the result of your indiscretions. Do you understand what those indiscretions are?"

"Yes, sir. I should attend you as soon as I know you've asked for me."

"You must understand there are consequences to your actions, should you choose not to comply with a request."

"Yes, sir. I understand."

"I carry out corporal punishment on my boys, as you know. Do you understand the need for punishment?"

Alec's head was spinning, fighting against the desire stoking in his body as he tried to understand what the fuck Hamilton was talking about. Hamilton went to the cupboard behind the sofa. Alec couldn't see what Hamilton held in his hand when he came to stand next to him, but he sensed something.

"Do you understand the need for punishment?"

"Yes… Master." Alec had no intention of allowing his boss to punish him, but his master was a different person altogether, regardless of the fact they were the same man. They were crossing the line from the office to their personal lives. Hamilton hadn't said it, but Alec felt it in his manner. *My boys…* he was talking about Brendon, Dylan, and Sebastian, not Michael or Mehmet. Hamilton's tone of voice changed when he spoke about his houseboys.

"You will refrain from making any sound. Do I make myself clear?"

"Yes, sir, what—"

Fucking hell!

Whatever Alec had been expecting it wasn't that. His ass cheek burned in completely the wrong way. Another one. Alec bit down on his lip to stop the stream of profanity that threatened to burst from his gaping mouth. The intensity increased after the first few blows. After ten, Alec's legs started to shake and it was harder to hold back the whimpering. He wanted to drop to his knees, beg Hamilton to forgive him, kiss his feet, suck his cock, have the entire office fuck his ass, anything but more of this. On and on it continued, his ass was on fire, his back clammy with sweat.

"Please, Master. I'm so sorry," Alec mumbled. He fought back tears, not from the pain but from the burn of shame that punishment was necessary. His own thoughts mocked him—*not such a beautiful boy now.*

Hamilton's hand smoothed over Alec's back, calming him, but the blows continued and Alec zoned out. He concentrated on the feel of Hamilton's hand caressing his cool skin far away from the burn and sting of his ass cheeks. His breathing settled and his muscles relaxed as he let go of a long, deep sigh.

"Good boy, Alec," he heard Hamilton whisper. "Always such a good boy."

It took a moment for Alec to realize it had stopped and Hamilton was leaning over his back, holding him around the waist. It felt good and he moved into the touch. "Thank you, Master."

"Get dressed, Alec. I'm afraid we don't have time for anything else."

It was a good job they didn't. Alec's ass smarted as he pulled on his clothes. Even bending to tie his shoes had the undesirable effect of chaffing the oversensitive skin of his ass cheeks. As the door closed behind him Alec took a deep breath, he'd never been so relieved to get back to the bustle of the main office.

Alec winced as he sat at his desk.

"What's wrong with you?" Chloe's voice dripped with sarcasm. "Get a spanking for being a bad boy and not running when the boss-man called?"

"*Fuck. Off.*"

Her face fell. "Alec, I didn't mean anything by it. It was a stupid joke. I'm sorry."

He looked up to see genuine concern. She was a decent enough friend really. The last few weeks had been weird for all of them. "I'm just... I'm not a doormat, okay?"

"Okay. No more bossman jokes. Brownie's honor."

"You were never a Brownie."

"True, but I was in the Girl's Brigade so you can trust me." She grinned and Alec had to smile. This morning he'd been on top of the world, now everything was a bit of a mess. The only thing he could do was suck cock as best as he could this evening. Suck his way back into Hamilton's good books.

Friday mornings in the office really dragged.

"How's your backside?"

After the lunch break Hamilton had summoned Alec again. "Tender, sir." Much improved considering it had only been a few hours since his punishment but even now, sitting on his heels at Hamilton's feet, a light throb still burned his ass cheeks.

"Have you learned your lesson, Alec?"

"Yes, sir. I am to respond immediately to your requests."

"Good. What I want now, is to know exactly what you were doing fraternizing with another member of my team in the stairwell. Think very carefully before you answer. I will not tolerate lies."

"He was comforting me, after Chloe was cruel, and then I was comforting him because he thinks his girlfriend is cheating on him."

"Was it sexual?"

"No, sir. He did mention to me that he's had experience with men but he wasn't hitting on me or anything."

Hamilton looked like he was thinking. "How was Chloe cruel?"

"She didn't mean anything. I was being over-sensitive. She was teasing me about you."

"I see. And Tom Parsons is often kind to you?"

"We've been friends from the day I started here, sir. He's the one who told me the position was going on your team back last year."

"Then we have a lot to thank Tom for. I want you to suck his cock."

"Sir? But he's straight… and a friend."

Hamilton frowned. "Are you questioning me so soon after your punishment, Alec?"

"No, I just don't know how he would let me."

"It's very simple, Alec. You get him alone and you say, 'I want to suck your cock for being so good to me.'"

"Right. I can do that. I think." There was no way in hell he'd be able to go through with it. Another ass whacking was definitely on the cards.

"Off you go then."

"Now?"

"Act upon requests immediately. Do I really have to bring out the paddle to remind you?"

Paddle? Is that what the fucking thing was? "No, sir." Alec got to his feet and hovered. "I'll get right on it."

"I'd like evidence of it, just to make sure."

"Such as?"

"You have a cell phone. I want to be able to see that you are on your knees with a cock in your mouth. Tom's legs should be identifiable from his suit pants."

Oh, shit. Not only ask Tom if I can suck his cock, but also ask him to take a photo of me doing him. "I guess I'll be on my way then."

"You have an hour. You know Tom leaves early on a Friday."

Alec could have sworn Hamilton chuckled as he left the office. *Ha-fucking-ha.* He could do this. Tom had already said he was open to it. Maybe he'd even been hinting at it. Alec could at least say that was the reason for his sudden interest.

Sure enough, Tom was tidying his desk for the weekend. "Tom have you got a minute?"

"Sure, what's up?"

Alec couldn't look at him, couldn't say anything, he just walked off, and thankfully Tom followed. He made his way to the fourth-floor bathrooms. Because they were generally deserted, Alec had always used the floor for wanking—it made sense to use it for blow-jobs too.

"Alec, are you okay?" As usual the bathroom was empty. He shoved Tom into a cubicle and locked the door. "What are you doing?"

Alec spun them both around so that Tom was against the door. He handed him his phone. "Hold this." And pulled at Tom's belt.

"Fuck, Alec stop, what's *wrong* with you?"

"I want to suck your cock for being so good to me, and I want you to take a photo of me doing it."

"Is this a joke? Is Chloe going to burst in here—you didn't tell her did you?"

"Shut the fuck up, Tom, and take the picture." Alec sat on the toilet seat, pulled out Tom's cock, and wrapped his mouth around it.

"Fucking hell, man. Sweet Jesus, you're really doing it."

Tom's cock hardened nicely under Alec's attention.

"Take the damn picture."

"Picture, right. Kinky."

Alec got back to work and Tom sighed, relaxing into the process. It was a nice enough cock, slightly unusual flavor that he put down to Tom's shower gel or perhaps deodorant; it was a bit perfumed. Each time Alec looked up, Tom clicked the camera. He was biting his lip furiously to hold back the sounds that kept escaping. Alec was feeling pleased with himself by the time Tom pulled out his cock.

"Hey, I was enjoying that," Alec complained.

"So was I. A little too much, to be honest. Sorry to steal your thunder—"

Tom pushed Alec to his feet, leaned over the bowl, and finished himself.

Alec watched with some regret Tom's cum spurt into the water. "I… appreciate the… thought, Alec. But… you didn't have… to do that."

"I wanted to."

Tom cleaned up and tucked himself away. He leaned forward and kissed Alec on the lips. "I've got a girlfriend, Alec. A cheating bitch of a girlfriend but that doesn't mean *I* play the field. We're friends, okay? But no benefits."

"Gotcha." Alec tried not to let the relief color his reply. The last thing he wanted at work was added complications.

"And I am not gonna reciprocate, so don't even think about it."

"No problem. Can I have my phone?"

"Oh, yeah. Let's have a look at the pics." They scrolled through the few shots. "Fuck, don't you dare show these to anyone. You can tell that's me."

"You think? It's just a cock and a pair of legs."

"People in this building will know that is *my* cock down your throat. It's fucking hot though. Email them to me?"

"Oh, I get it. I'm not allowed to do it again but you'll use the evidence as wanking inspiration."

"That about sums it up. But if the wanking is really good, I might let you do it again." Tom pinched Alec's ass, gave a last kiss, this time with a bit of tongue, and opened the door. "You're sexy, Alec, I'll give you that. Email me the photos." And he was gone.

Alec ran through the bizarre chain of events that led to him handing over photos of him sucking his friend's cock to his boss. There had been a few close calls with the truth today too, but it seemed that it could only be considered in jest.

"You look like you're enjoying yourself," Hamilton said, scrolling through the pictures.

"He was a bit shocked. I was trying not to laugh at the look on his face. It certainly made it interesting."

"I'm very pleased with you, Alec. That you would do something so against your natural instincts because I asked you to."

"I'd do anything for you, Master."

"That remains to be seen but for the moment I am more than satisfied. Are you ready to leave?"

"Five minutes to tidy my desk?"

"Off you go then."

Alec was surprised to see Tom still there. Chloe had left and most of the office was empty.

"Alec, I'm sorry if you thought I was coming on to you earlier, telling you about... stuff."

"That's not why I did it, Tom. I don't want this to get weird. Let's just leave it at that, yeah?"

"Okay, that's good. As long as you're sure everything's okay."

"I'm sure."

Tom walked around the desk and pulled Alec into a hug. "You're a good guy, Alec." he pulled Alec's head onto his shoulder and kissed his neck. "Thank you, buddy. You made me feel good about myself again. I love you for that."

"You're welcome."

"Cuddling again?"

"Mr. Hamilton," Tom spluttered. "I, uh..."

"Alec told me."

The color drained from Tom's face and Alec tried to stifle a snort. "He did?"

"About your girlfriend. I hope things settle out."

"Right, yes. One of those things I guess. He's good. A good friend,

Alec is," Tom blustered. "I'll see you Monday."

Alec had never seen Tom move so fast as when he high-tailed it out of the office in that moment. "You are so cruel."

Hamilton gave Alec a wink. "And you, apparently, are good. You haven't tidied your desk."

"Huh? Oh, Tom… I'll do it now."

"I'll meet you at the car. Don't be long. We've a busy night ahead."

Busy indeed. Alec was one cock back into Hamilton's good books. The light throb in his ass cheeks reminded him there would be a few more to go.

Party Time

Everything was set for the guests to arrive. Alec sat at the dining room table with Hamilton as he laid out a selection of toys, condoms, and lube. Alec was beginning to appreciate the design and layout of Hamilton's apartment. Everything about the public rooms, the vast open-plan space that his guests used during parties, catered to sex. The seating was of varying heights and levels of firmness in the most sumptuous leathers and velvets, with plenty of lumbar support cushions to hand. Overly wide armchairs, benches that served the dining area as well as seating areas, footstools, chaises, and long deep sofas created semi private areas which became one large expanse with the minimum of fuss. Hard surfaces were reflective, mirrored, or highly polished steel to provide a view of the action wherever anyone looked.

The lighting was subtle and completely adjustable to spotlight some areas and leave others in darkness, or lit by the two-foot high, ten-foot wide open fire built into one wall. Even the barstools were of different heights and shaped to support the torso while being fucked from behind. Several low tables were upholstered, and Alec wouldn't have been surprised to find them designed specifically to accommodate the weight of several men. Muted colors of grays, teals, and damson purples matched the art on the white walls and accented the occasional rugs scattered over highly polished wooden floors so dark they looked almost black. Yes, Alec more than appreciated the comforts; they were becoming an accepted part of life.

The boys were getting excited. They lounged and crawled over each other in all their nakedness on the sofa like young animals. Dylan already sported a decent erection and it made Alec's own cock ache.

"You can join them, if you want to."

"I'd rather sit with you, Master," Alec said. A shiver ran over him when Hamilton stroked his arm.

"There will be a steady stream of guests this evening but no more than twelve in total. Finnola will be visiting to see Dylan. She's the only guest I expect you not to interact with unless someone specifically refuses your service."

"All the cocks—got it. She won't ask me to do anything will she? I wouldn't know how."

"She may want to play with you a little but you needn't worry, her tastes run very much to Dylan's specialities."

"Isn't Dylan gay?"

"He enjoys his occasional dalliance with the ladies but his heart belongs to Brendon."

"Master." Dylan leapt across the room and fell at Hamilton's feet with complete subservience. "Master, my heart belongs to you."

"Ah, such a good boy. Thank you, Dylan. You know I don't mind you having feelings for Brendon."

"But my heart and my body, Master, belong to you."

Wow. There was such truth in the statement it made Alec shiver. Could Alec claim to have such devotion? He'd been playing this game for a few weeks now and while this was only his second party he'd sucked plenty of cocks here and at work for Hamilton, gotten to his knees because it was what Hamilton requested of him, and fucked because Hamilton wanted to see his cock in another's ass. But there were still lines between them somehow. Alec used the term *master* and he understood it to an extent, but seeing Dylan, his body so relaxed in that pose, a sense of peace radiating from him, Alec realized he had a lot more to learn.

Hamilton allowed Dylan to stand and spent some time lavishing affection on Dylan's cock. Oh, yes, Dylan definitely loved Hamilton. He'd seen Brendon give Dylan a blowjob and his reactions were nothing like those he expressed now—involuntary, lost in the moment responses that ended too soon with the doorbell. Hamilton continued to stroke Dylan for a moment to calm him. "Good boy, Dylan. I'll finish that for you later, sweetheart."

"Thank you so much, Master."

"Take your place. Make me proud."

Dylan scooted back to the end of the longest low table. The three of them lined up like statues, on their knees, hands in their laps, heads bowed. It was an imposing sight and Alec's cock started to swell.

"Should I join them?"

"Not yet, I need to plug you first. Let me open the door."

Hmm. Alec had an idea what that meant. Hamilton had used a butt plug on him a few times, and dildos, but only during sex. He stood and pushed the dining room chair back into position against the table. He may not have to join the other boys, but he should at least be standing to greet the guests.

"Alec, how delightful." Dicky brushed his arm and let it trail down over Alec's ass. As he turned to see Hamilton, his fingers slipped between Alec's ass cheeks and rubbed over his pucker. "Is Alec's ass open tonight, Hamilton? You know I want to be his first."

"Dicky, unhand that boy this instant." Hamilton took the sting from his words with a chuckle. "I can see exactly what you're doing. There's a mirror on the wall behind you, you old dog."

"Ah…" Dicky leaned into Alec affectionately. "Caught in the act. You don't mind a little fondling do you, Alec?"

"My only wish is to serve my Master, Dicky."

"I brought Jules. He refused to be left at home."

Alec had been vaguely aware of Jules saying hello to the boys in his own way—a kiss and a quick suck on the cock of each, and now he made his way toward Alec. "Hey, you. Can't call you, new kid anymore. Fancy a fuck?" He pulled Alec into a snog.

Alec didn't respond, he didn't have permission. Jules slipped to his knees, took hold of Alec's cock and pulled back the foreskin to lick over the head. He sucked hard a few times and let it go. "It's kind of my thing," he said with a grin. "If I'm sharing someone else's turf it's only polite to say hello properly."

"You are beyond hope," Dicky said, slapping Jules's ass. "Take your position before I change my mind and send you home."

"Yes, Master." The tone of voice and the way Jules slid down Dicky's body to kiss his cock through his pants made Alec rock hard. Damn, he just oozed sex appeal. Dicky was definitely breathing heavily. Jules turned on his heel and started to strip off.

"Dicky, keep an eye on things while I plug Alec for the evening. We don't want any incidents of accidental penetration, now do we?"

Dicky frowned. Alec was more than happy for there to be no chance of *accidental penetration*. "It's damned unfair to have something so pretty, unavailable."

"I promise you, Alec will suck your cock with pleasure. Won't you, Alec?"

"Absolutely, Master. Dicky, yours was the first cock I sucked on my first evening. I'm always happy to service you, sir."

"Why that's right. And very nice it was too. I still want to fuck you though, lad. But I can wait."

"Thank you, sir."

Hamilton led Alec into the bedroom. "Dicky's a cheeky old devil. You make sure he doesn't whip out the plug just for a few thrusts when I'm not looking. On the bed, Alec."

"Would he do that?"

Alec crawled onto all fours and spread his knees, presenting his ass. Hamilton put a small plug on the bed next to Alec's knee and pushed a couple of lubed fingers into his hole, wriggling them around and pushing the lube deep inside.

"He thinks I'm playing not offering you for service. I haven't had a chance to explain to him properly. Once he knows the reason, he wouldn't go against it but at the moment, it's a game."

"What should I do if he tries it?" Alec winced as Hamilton leaned on a sore ass cheek.

"Sorry, darling, still a little tender?"

"It's not too bad now."

Hamilton pushed the plug into place with a few thrusts. "If you get the chance, stand up and ask him for the plug. He'll be too embarrassed to refuse you. Don't worry. I'll speak to him this evening. Hopefully, before he gets any ideas."

Alec was grateful of the plug's protection. Hamilton kissed him a little and then guided him back to the main room. The boys, now including Jules, were waiting as before. Dicky had undressed and taken a seat on the sofa.

"Join the boys, Alec. You are not to leave this room, even if it gets busy. Any special requests will be communicated by me personally."

"I understand, Master."

The boys shuffled to give Alec a space between Jules and Brendon. He would have been much happier next to Sebastian. Hamilton and Dicky moved to the far end of the room and Alec hoped it was to discuss the no-fucking policy.

"Hey, Alec," Jules whispered, knocking against him. "How about we get behind the sofa later and take out that plug so I can thank you for the great fuck the other week?"

Brendon reached across to push him away. "You can fuck right off, Jules. If anyone fucks the pet it's me, so get your ass in line."

"Pet?"

"Alec is Master's favorite. It used to be Sebastian, but he's being replaced."

"Brendon, shut up," Alec said, sitting straight to look down at him. "You really are a first-class prick."

Brendon scowled, but the other three burst into fits of laughter.

"Is this something I should be concerned with?" Hamilton said, looking up from his conversation with Dicky. "Brendon?"

"No, Master, we're just playing." Brendon reached back and pinched Alec's tender ass cheek making him jump.

"I'll get you for that," Alec whispered.

"Counting on it." Brendon winked. His grin confirmed he really was only playing, but the remark stung.

The little squabble caused Alec to miss the arrival of several men. Naked men. They stood around, chatting and laughing with each other, and helped themselves to drinks. Alec retained his pose, sat back on his haunches, hands in his lap, head slightly bowed. It was easier than trying to follow what was going on. It wasn't long before a man touched his shoulder. Alec stood and followed him to one of the armchairs, where the man deposited an empty tumbler on a side table and sat down. He didn't look much older than Hamilton, certainly only early thirties. He was a nice-looking guy, slightly built, and his hair in the low light looked tinged with copper flecks. Alec knelt at his feet and the man threaded his fingers through Alec's hair and pulled his head down to meet his semi-hard cock. No words of introduction or instruction, so Alec opened his mouth and began to suckle the end. The man let go of his head. "Just get the job done, boy. There are asses to fuck and I need to get the first load out the way. Helps my stamina, don't you know."

Fine, if that's how he wanted it. Alec added a hand and got on with it. It wasn't pretty or sensual but the guy sprayed into his mouth soon enough. He started to lick over the spent cock.

"That's enough, I don't need a nursemaid. Bring me another whiskey."

"Right away, sir."

What a tosser. And Alec could still taste his cum. Not his best experience and not a good first for the evening. He found the whiskey decanter and headed back to his client, the fucker. The man didn't even acknowledge him, just held out the glass for filling and then waved him away. Alec refilled a few more glasses on his way back to the bar. Dicky was waiting for him. Great. All he needed was an incident of accidental penetration. What a perfect fucking day. Hamilton appeared at his side.

"Alec, take Dicky into my room for a little private time, there's a good boy."

Alec wanted to cry, but he said, "Of course, Master." Hamilton smoothed over his back and Alec remembered to breathe.

With the door closed Dicky sat on the sofa at the end of Hamilton's bed. "Sit with me, Alec."

The mix of the butt plug and the spanking made him wince slightly. "Thank you, sir."

"You don't need to be afraid, Alec. I've brought you here to apologize. Hamilton has explained that you won't be moving into the pool with the other boys. I promise to keep my hands out of your ass from now on."

Alec let go of a deep breath he didn't realize he'd been holding and his body relaxed. Dicky pulled him in for a cuddle. "Thank you so much, Dicky. I really like you. I'm happy for you to touch but Master says no fucking."

"I know. It explains why you're such a sweet boy. Hamilton is very fond of you. I will touch and be cheeky, because that's me, but you're perfectly safe. I take Hamilton's rules seriously, we all do. Don't be afraid to speak out for your own safety."

"Who was that man I just serviced? I know I'm not supposed to ask, but he wasn't very nice to me."

"He'll warm up as the evening goes on. He has a very stressful job, working for very unpleasant people. It's why he's here. An evening of good, hard fucking is the cure to many ills. Don't judge him too harshly."

"I've so much to learn. Is that why Hamilton has these parties, to offer stress release to important people?"

"Not the only reason, but one of them I guess. I for one, have little stress these days, other than keeping Jules satisfied." They chuckled together and Alec thought it wouldn't be so bad to be fucked by Dicky; he was kind of sweet really. "Now, what say you to a nice blow-job for this aging cock?"

"I'd love to, Dicky." Someone that would appreciate Alec's efforts at least. He laid the old man along the sofa and crawled over him with his ass toward Dicky's face.

"I say, Alec, do you think I'm allowed to play with your butt plug a little?"

"I would think so. It's just cocks that aren't allowed in. Master often lets the boys prepare me with one finger, but no more. I could ask for you?"

"Maybe it could be our little secret?"

Alec chuckled. Cheeky indeed. "Okay, Dicky. And you are allowed to touch my cock of course." Not that Alec was expecting a blowjob from him, but a little friction wouldn't go amiss. He should have known Dicky would be good. Alec gasped around his mouth full of cock as Dicky spread his ass cheeks and ran his tongue around the edge of the butt plug—he sucked, nipped and licked Alec's balls and shaft, and nudged the plug with his nose. Alec could barely concentrate on what he was doing, it was all very one sided until Dicky stopped his torture and rested his head.

"You're a wonderful boy, Alec, wonderful. Aah… just like that. Good boy, you know how I like it." Dicky was nothing, if not good for morale. Alec happily swallowed his offering and thoroughly cleaned his spent cock. "Magnificent," Dicky said. He reached up to kiss Alec's ass cheeks. "Now be a good boy and help me off my back. Bit of a stranded beetle like this I'm afraid."

Alec heaved him to his feet and they rejoined the party. It was all a bit of a blur from then on. One cock after another, thankfully with some wanting to come over him rather than down his throat, and most just needing to be sucked hard so they could fuck again. He had his five minutes with Finnola when she breezed through the room and stopped to fondle his balls, stroke his cock, and scrape gloriously sharp fingernails over his thighs, before disappearing with Dylan.

Alec sat back on his heels, waiting to be called. A tap on his shoulder and he turned to see his first jerk of a client. "Another whiskey?"

"Certainly, sir." Alec tried to keep in mind what Dicky had said. He smiled as he found the man back in the same chair. He did look different. He was lounging comfortably, his head resting back against the chair. This time he smiled as he held out his glass." Come and sit with me a moment."

Alec returned the whiskey decanter to its place on the bar and went to kneel on the floor.

"No." The man sat up straighter and patted his lap. The great thing about Hamilton's armchairs was their breadth—wide enough for you to sit to one side or between the legs of someone rather than perching on their thighs, and with arms low enough to throw your legs over comfortably. Alec slipped onto the chair and let his ass fall to one side of the guy's hips. "I'm Adam. I'm sorry I didn't say much earlier."

"You don't have to apologize, sir."

"I know." Adam was stroking Alec's back and it felt nice. Sensual nice. Sexy nice. The butt plug was starting to chafe and had been pressing against his sweet spot on and off all night. The way he'd sat in the chair was adding pressure. The cool whiskey glass rested on Alec's knee and started a slow, teasing path along Alec's thigh. It brushed his cock before making the return journey. "I was pissed off because you weren't in the pool for fucking. As soon as I saw you, with your head bowed, I wanted you."

"Thank you, sir."

"I still want you." Sure enough, Alec felt the cock swell against his hip. Adam chugged the contents of the whiskey glass and placed it on the side table. His free hand went straight to Alec's cock and started to tug in firm strokes.

An ice-cold shower was what Alec could do with right now. He had to close his eyes, take his mind away from the building pressure in his balls.

"All this fucking going on and you've not been able to take part. Your ass must be burning with the feel of that butt plug. I think what you'd really like is for me to bend you over the table and fuck the living daylights out of you."

Too close to the truth. Alec bit back a whimper as he fought the spiral in his guts which threatened to overwhelm as Adam slipped a tongue around his ear and filled his mind with hot, sweet words of lust and need.

A kiss on the other side of his neck and Alec opened his eyes to see Hamilton holding out his hand. He lifted Alec from Adam's thighs and led him to the central chaise and laid him across it. "Such a beautiful boy," Hamilton whispered between kisses over Alec's chest. "Tell me what you want, Alec and it's yours." A lap of Hamilton's tongue over his cock and this time he didn't hold on to the sound, he let it roll from his throat like a growl.

"You, I want you. Fuck me, Master, please."

A short burn as Hamilton removed the plug. Alec felt empty for just a moment before the pressure of hot, slick cock filled him. He could feel Hamilton's hips pressing against him as he pulled his legs farther toward his chest. "Suck the cock, Alec." Alec opened his eyes to see Adam kneeling over him, cock just an inch from his lips and he opened his mouth to receive it. Filled at both ends, just what he wanted. He sucked, swirled, and savored Adam's cock while Hamilton pounded into his ass, beating him into submission all over again. With his mouth full, he couldn't beg for the release he craved. Sudden suction over his cock made him jump but Hamilton's soft, gentle hands steadied him. "Relax into it, Alec. Almost time."

It was too much. It seemed as though a hundred hands were on his body, stroking and probing, tweaking his nipples and kneading his balls. The tight, wet, heat increased over his cock as it slipped deeper into someone's throat and he tried to cry out, but it only let the cock in his mouth deeper into his throat. And his sweet spot, over and over, massaged by the head of Hamilton's cock and he couldn't, he just couldn't hold on any longer but he had to. No permission. No more punishment. Alec was a good boy, a beautiful boy. He didn't care if he was the master's favorite or the boss's fuck toy—he *wanted* to be, needed Hamilton to be pleased with him more than anything in the world, and he was so close to fucking it all up.

"Come for me, Alec."

The magic words spiraled with his climax. A cry tore from his chest, around the cock in his mouth. On and on, the orgasm seemed to sweep through his whole body. He sucked hard on Adam's cock and the man spilled down his throat as Hamilton emptied into him. Amazing.

Adam withdrew and stroked Alec's face. Alec returned a tired, sated smile. Jules dived in for a sloppy smooch. "You taste good," he teased and pinched Alec's cheek.

And then there was Hamilton, who stroked his chest with a firm hand as he lowered his legs until his feet touched the floor. He pulled Alec to sit upright, "I think you need your bed."

"Thank you, Master, I am sleepy."

Dicky surprised him with a kiss on the lips and a wink before Jules dragged him off, feigning lack of attention. The party was at an end, clothes were donned once more; Brendon, Dylan, and Sebastian had left, no doubt already in the bath.

"Thank you, Alec. I hope to see you again." Adam handed Alec a large tip and brushed his hair back from his face. "Seeing you come like that just makes me want you even more. If I believed in fate or love at first sight, I'd say this was it. I can only hope one day I'll find a partner like you."

"Thank you, sir. I don't know what to say."

"Call me, Adam. Can I have a kiss?" Alec nodded and Adam drew him up into his arms to meet his lips. A hand slipped behind his neck and pulled him close, a hint of tongue, the taste of whiskey, and it was over. "Perfect," Adam sighed. "As I knew it would be. Good night, Alec."

"Goodbye, Adam."

Hamilton pulled Alec to his feet and through to the bathroom. After a quick shower, they curled together in bed with tender kisses and soft caresses. "You're so special, Alec, I can't begin to tell you."

"As are you."

"Adam has taken a liking to you."

"He said he loved me. Love at first sight. That's not real."

"Are you sure?"

Alec thought about it. Thought about the first time he'd seen Hamilton. Infatuated, yes, but love? Alec loved him now, knew it without any question, but it had grown over time. Months of devotion topped off with these last few weeks of crazy sex and life-changing experiences, and Hamilton had been there for it all. "I think you can feel something like love, but it has no foundation."

"Maybe that's what it is, then." Hamilton kissed Alec's forehead. "Sleep now. We have a busy day tomorrow."

"We do?"

"Yes, very busy. It's a surprise."

Hamilton's surprises were always the best. They ended in killer orgasms that left Alec's body in a restful mass of jello haze. He nestled closer and Hamilton wrapped an arm around his hip. A sigh of pure contentment escaped Alec's lips. *Just perfect.*

Bands

It was sunny and warm. A light breeze came from the open floor-length windows of the living room where Alec and Sebastian canoodled on the large super-soft rug. It wasn't a penthouse apartment; other buildings overlooked so it was possible to be watched from outside. It added to the fuse of passion from their grinding bodies.

Sebastian was undeniably cute and deliciously sexy. His slight, boyish frame, only five-six with tiny hips, belied his manly capabilities and a cock that matched Alec's in length but had greater girth. He pressed all of Alec's hot buttons in just the right way.

"I'd choose you as lover, Alec," Sebastian whispered. "Even without Master." Alec groaned as Sebastian wrapped a hand around both their cocks for added friction. "I wish we were allowed to come, just for us."

"They're at it again."

Alec and Sebastian sprang apart like naughty children at Brendon's taunt. Tight balls and throbbing cocks gave them away when Hamilton appeared.

"Leave them alone, Brendon. You get up to plenty of mischief behind my back. Don't think I don't know."

"But, Master. I would never come without your permission."

"And neither have they. If they want to torment themselves into a frenzy that can't be satisfied, what business is it of yours?" Brendon dropped his head. "Well? And are you really telling me that you weren't sucking Dylan's cock this morning before breakfast?"

"No, Master. I'm sorry, Master."

"I don't know what's got into to you lately. I will punish you if this surliness continues. It's very trying."

"Forgive me, Master."

"Bend over the table. Sebastian come and fuck the attitude out of this boy, before I back-hand him. Don't you dare huff, Brendon. I'm tired of your insolence."

Brendon draped himself over the low table in the seating area. He really didn't look happy. Alec had noted before that Brendon didn't like Sebastian fucking him and he only touched Sebastian if he was told to. For guys that lived together it must make things difficult, especially considering their bizarre lifestyle.

Sebastian launched into a deep thrusting action but it seemed mechanical compared to the interlude of a few moments ago with Alec. Brendon put in no effort but it was obvious from his breathing and the way his hands clenched the table he was getting plenty out of it. It seemed strange to Alec that Brendon could fuck old men and strangers with such passion and yet a sweet little thing like Sebastian had him feigning disinterest.

Hamilton dropped the morning paper on the table. He didn't seem impressed by the show. Brendon yelped as Hamilton pulled him off the table by his hair. "Your manner suggests you are not taking pleasure from my request, Brendon. Is this so?"

"No, Master… I only want to please you."

"Then please me or god help me I'll have Sebastian fuck you all day every day until you *do* enjoy it and without another hand touching you. Not even my own."

"Please. Master, I can be good."

"Then show me."

When Hamilton let go his hair, Brendon transformed into a writhing sex fiend. It continued even when Hamilton left the room for a few moments. Whatever had been bugging Brendon seemed to flow away with the rising tide in his body. Hamilton returned with a large dildo and placed it on the table. "When you get close Sebastian, fuck him with this until you're able to continue. Keep up the pace. I want to see that boy squirm with need at your hand, regardless of how long it takes."

"Yes, Master." Sebastian seemed to put a little more effort into his duties with that.

"Alec, join me at the table." Alec knelt to kiss Hamilton's cock before taking a seat. "I want to talk to you about your training."

"I want to be the best I can for you, Master."

"You're doing very well overall. Aside from our little incident yesterday your responses to commands at this point are excellent."

"Thank you, Master."

"Your cock sucking is coming along very nicely but I think a more concentrated effort may be necessary for you to read different needs much sooner."

"Do I take too long?"

"It's more that you don't seem to understand, without being told, whether a client wants something quick, or something more skilful. It's an art, don't be discouraged."

"And how do I learn?"

"Experience. I'd like you to spend an evening at the club. You can easily take twenty or thirty cocks in a few hours and although your jaw will undoubtedly ache it will be worth the pay off."

"You want me to suck other men's cocks at the club so that I can be better at sucking yours?"

"That sums it up, darling."

Alec was surprised to find this wasn't a problem. He relished the thought of being able to better please Hamilton and he couldn't deny the buzz he received just at the thought of Hamilton handing him out. "Okay. You'll tell me who?"

"Ah, I knew you were perfect. I'll supervise. Don't worry. We'll go to the club a little later, but first shopping." Hamilton winked, his eyes sparkled. "I'll need to get you something to wear."

Alec raised surprised eyebrows. "Wear? I'm usually naked."

"That's fine for private parties and work functions but this is a public club. For your first visit it may be best to cover you up just a little."

"Public, as in anyone can walk off the street kind of club?"

"Absolutely. Although we have our own tables on a more exclusive floor. But it's true you could find yourself giving a blowjob to the barista who serves your coffee at Starbucks. Is that a problem?"

"Not if it's what you want of me, Master. I'd suck his cock *in* Starbucks if you requested it."

Hamilton stroked Alec's face in that wonderful way that made him weak at the knees. "Good boy, just what I like to hear." They both turned at a particularly load moan from Brendon. "He's warming up nicely, don't you think?"

"Sebastian is good with that dildo." Sebastian flashed a heart-winning smile at Alec and his breath caught in his chest. Fuck, he couldn't crush on a houseboy, could he? And how did that even work when he was so obsessed with Hamilton anyway?

"Seems to me you'd like to be on the receiving end of his attentions yourself."

"Only if you wish it, Master."

"Right answer, good boy. Keep it up Sebastian. I'm going for a shower. I want that boy begging by the time I return."

"Yes, Master. I think I may be too, if that's okay."

Hamilton chuckled as Alec watched his delectable ass disappear through the door.

101

Alec took his turn to shower and change while Hamilton fussed over Dylan. He was starting to feel ignored when Hamilton called him into the bedroom.

"You've forgotten something, darling." Hamilton waved a butt plug in the air.

"I don't understand."

"We're going out together for the afternoon on a boys day. I have to mark you. Drop your pants and kneel on the bed."

Alec hesitated for only a moment. As he crawled into position, Hamilton almost purred. "I think you need a reward for being so good. Dylan, come and lick my boy's ass."

Alec jolted as a tongue ran over his crack. Firm hands pushed his still tender ass cheeks apart and a strong tongue pushed into him. The tongue fucked and licked and sucked and drove Alec to the very edge of distraction until he was rocking back against it, desperate to feel more inside him.

"I can't let you come, Alec. The plug will be too painful. But later you can come over and over for me."

"Thank you, Master." The words fell out of Alec's mouth without thought.

"Dylan, heel." The tongue disappeared and slicked fingers replaced it. "The extra lube will make you more comfortable. Are you ready?"

"Yes, please."

"Ah, my wonderful boy. You'll enjoy wearing this today. Every step will make you think of me inside your ass claiming you, making you mine."

As the plug slipped inside, Alec thought he would come. The idea of Hamilton being inside him all day was dizzying. Much like Brendon's howls in the other room from Sebastian's steady fucking. Alec breathed through it and the desire gradually settled.

"Get dressed, darling. I'll just finish the boys and we're ready."

Alec forced his hard cock back into his pants. Every movement rippled through his insides with a spike of heat and lust. He'd be a quivering mass of need before they hit the car. He watched Hamilton smooth and pet the boys, Brendon still trembling from what must have been a killer orgasm. He settled them into their room with food, a pile of DVDs, access to Hamilton's Netflix account, and promises that if they were very good, they could visit the club later.

The early lunch was a trial in patience and restraint. Sitting in the Ritz, silver service and the flush of desire obvious on his face, Alec wanted to die of shame. Hamilton lapped up his desperate noises and taunted Alec by toeing his cock through his pants under the table until he broke. "Please," Alec whispered trying to not to lean forward and push the plug further inside. "I have to…"

"Tell me what you need, Alec, and I will get it for you."

"I want you. To… fuck me. Please." Alec grabbed Hamilton's hand across the table. "Now."

Hamilton called over a waiter. "A room for an hour."

Alec trembled in the elevator, embarrassed at the look on his face. He was stripping off his clothes before the door to the vast room closed and he fell over the back of the nearest chair. "Fuck me. I can't wait anymore. Just do it."

"Patience, Alec. I gave you permission to ask for what you needed not order me to give it to you. You'll see to my needs first."

Alec peeled himself off the chair with a groan and fell to his knees in front of Hamilton. His hands shook as he pulled down the zipper and freed the rock-hard cock. The musky smell drew his lips and he sucked the head into his mouth. Oh, but he loved the taste of that cock, so distinct, the best flavor. He sucked, licked, and lapped over the head and all along the shaft but it only stoked the fire in his belly. He didn't realize he could be so turned on without coming. "Please," he whimpered.

"Back over the chair. Spread your legs nice and wide."

Alec scrabbled, desperate to get into position to receive that cock up his ass. His knees buckled as Hamilton ripped the plug from him, the plunging cock forced them straight, his toes gripped the thick carpet, and a cry erupted from his throat. The pounding was fierce, rougher than before but he didn't care, he welcomed it crying "yes" with every thrust. He slipped his feet farther apart, dipped his back to allow the intrusion deeper. Hitting. Just. The right. Spot. Every. Time.

"I have to… please. Can I?" His words were muttered half thoughts. The fucking stopped as abruptly as it began, the plug replaced. "No," he begged. Alec turned on his knees and pulled at Hamilton's sleeve. "Anything, I'll do anything, please." He'd never felt so wild with passion, so out of control with desperation.

"Anything?"

"Yes, Master, just let me come."

Hamilton opened the door to the room. A young man entered. He seemed familiar. The waiter! Alec's mind wouldn't stay still, he didn't understand. The man started to strip.

"This is Max. You will suck him until he comes and then you will fuck him for your own release."

Max stood before him, semi-hard cock hanging in his face. Alec didn't wait for an invitation. The cock hardened in his mouth, bumping the back of his throat as he tried not to gag. The man wouldn't come like this. He'd be here all afternoon. Alec forced himself to focus, grasped firm ass cheeks in his hands and pulled, fucking his own throat, trying to suck at the same time. It was working. Max was losing his cool, rocking with him and grasping at his hair. Alec probed and fingered the rim of his hole.

"Yes," Max mumbled. "Push it in." There was resistance as Alec's dry digit tried to push past the muscle. "Do it, force it." With more pressure, it slipped inside. Max clenched his teeth together. "I like the pain. Fuck me dry with your fingers."

The concentration was excruciating but numbed Alec's own need enough to get the job done. Max erupted into the back of his throat as Alec struggled to swallow. Cum ran from his lips and down his chin. Max dropped to his knees and licked it from Alec's face before spinning around to present his ass.

"Remember," Hamilton said. "You asked for this. I will not remove the plug and you'll be sensitive after you've come."

Alec nodded, taking the condom and lube that Hamilton offered him. He pushed in a lubed finger. "No," Max said. "Lube yourself and push straight in. I want your cock to prise me open. Force it into me in one thrust and fuck as hard as you can."

Alec complied, noticing again how much more pleasure he gained by taking simple orders. It didn't take long and with the plug still inside his ass, Alec's climax verged on painful yet exquisite. He muffled his groan as he bit into the flesh of Max's back, unable to move for a few moments as the last shudders rocked through him. His breathing settled and Alec pulled out, getting rid of the condom. When he turned back, he saw Hamilton had taken his place and was thrusting into the young waiter with all his strength and a roughness that made Alec's eyes water. Hamilton met his gaze. "Get under him and suck him until he comes."

Crawling under Max, Alec understood what Hamilton said about the plug making him sore. It chaffed and rubbed over sensitized skin but he followed the instruction. His technique was improving, he thought, as he was able to spend more time appreciating the cock in his mouth. A lick, a suck, and a nibble before forcing it as far as it would go, trying to open his throat without gagging. That still needed practice despite the number he'd swallowed over the last few weeks. Alec let Max fill up his mouth with spunk again, swallowing it all this time, savoring the taste. Different to Hamilton's but still not unpleasant.

Hamilton was silent as he came. It was robotic, no emotion. It was so unlike him Alec wondered what the problem was. Max dressed quickly and left. Alec sat on the edge of the bed and started to dress. Hamilton walked swiftly toward him took him off guard with a hard slap around the face. Another followed, this time with the back of the hand.

"What did I do?" Alec felt tears flow. Not from pain but from the shock. How did he have it so wrong again after such a short time?

"You enjoyed fucking him too much. You save those orgasms, only for me. Do you understand? *Do you understand?*" Alec fell to his knees and hugged Hamilton's legs. It was an automatic response. He couldn't bear the anger aimed at him. Not irritation like Brendon had aroused earlier but real anger, which caused him to lash out rather than punish. It was wrong, Hamilton was wrong somehow, but yet it was Alec's fault.

"I'm so sorry. Please forgive me. Teach me, Master; show me how you want me to be. I want to be your good boy."

Hamilton's temper melted. He sat on the bed and pulled Alec into his arms, rocking him like a child, like the boys after they came for him, and Alec cried. He sobbed into Hamilton's chest, letting go of his confusion and appreciating the attention.

"I will always look after you, Alec. You're mine now."

"Yes. I want to be yours." And in that moment, it was the truth. Alec felt safe and oddly at peace despite the sting in his face and the bite in his ass. "Are you mine, Master?"

"I will always be here for you."

It wasn't the same. Alec needed to know that Hamilton was more his own than anyone else's, that there was a two-way street of some kind even if not as obvious as Alec would like. "But you'll still fuck other people?"

"Alec, I don't live a conventional life. I thought you understood that, I've tried to show you at least. It's as much my job as is it yours to fuck at work, but it's more than that for me. I like it. I like the buzz of taking someone new, of putting on a show, of having men at my feet sucking my cock. It's why I do, what I do. But I can promise that I'll never lie to you. I fuck other people, Alec. I'm not going to change. I fuck other people and so do you, but we still have something that is only for each other."

It wasn't an ideal answer, but it was enough to think about for now. "I'm only for you, Master."

"And I love that about you."

"I'm so glad you chose me to be your new boy."

"You are so much more, Alec, so much more."

A little kissing and a lot of cuddling later and Alec felt ready to face the world again. Hamilton whisked him through Savile Row for tailoring and Oxford Street for casual wear, subjecting him to preening and prodding to within an inch of his life at various stops along the way. He sighed as Hamilton dragged him to yet another doorway.

"Last one, darling. I promise."

With the door still closing, Alec felt the flush rush over his face. His jaw dropped. The store had looked so respectable from the outside.

"Ah, Mr. Hamilton. What can I show you today?"

"This is Alec. I'll need collar and cuffs, something special. Alec is not a puppy, Maurice, he's all my own."

"I understand."

Leather. There was so much leather, and rubber, and metal. Chains and cuffs and… Alec didn't know if he should look.

"See anything you like, Alec? Have a look around. I'll buy you whatever you want."

Alec felt too afraid to touch anything. He wandered the racks and shelves, letting his eyes drift over the merchandise. He couldn't begin to guess what half of it was for but he was very aware of the plug still wedged in his body and the hardness straining against the new Armani jeans Hamilton had insisted he change into.

"Sweetheart, come and see." Hamilton beamed as he lifted a half-inch gold choker and leash from its box. "It's perfect don't you think?" Hamilton unhooked the leash. "Kneel for me, Alec."

Alec's body complied with the order before he had a chance to think about what was really going on. *A fucking dog leash? Hamilton had just told the guy he wasn't a puppy and yet he handed over a god-damned leash. Stupid old man, as if Hamilton needed any encouragement.* Hamilton wriggled the chain over Alec's head and let it fall around his neck. It was heavy. Heavy enough to remember he was wearing it. Next came matching bracelets. He reached out his hands without prompting and Hamilton gave him the most beautiful smile Alec had yet seen. The gold chains hugged his wrists with little free room for them to move around. Thick flat gold links with no space between.

"Take off your sweater."

Again, Alec obeyed without thinking. It was such a relief not having to make decisions, not having to know how to react in unfamiliar situations. Far less stressful than meeting men at work or at Hamilton's parties, all he had to do was what Hamilton told him to do.

"Oh, they look lovely against his skin," Maurice said, clapping his hands together. Alec couldn't tell if the guy was camping it up or just excitable.

The chains did feel good though, comforting. The leash was freaking him out just a bit even though it still lay on the counter. Just the thought of it made him shudder, and Alec was pretty sure it wasn't in a good way.

"The perfect choice, Maurice, as always. Alec is in training. Maybe you would accept his service as reward for yours?"

"It would be an honor, Mr. Hamilton." Maurice bowed his head to him. "In the dressing room perhaps?"

Alec looked quickly at Hamilton. Was he really going to make him suck off this fat old man—in a store?

"Go along, Alec, I will be with you shortly." Alec started to stand but a firm hand held his shoulder. "I think it appropriate for you to stay on your knees."

Was this the next level of training? Alec knew enough of Hamilton, how he worked, to consider rolling with it. The outcome usually outweighed the dubious beginning and Alec was yet to be disappointed.

By the time Alec got to the dressing room on hands and knees, the shriveled cock of Maurice hung in full view beneath his huge belly. When Maurice turned to look at him, it started to show signs of life. "Beautiful," Maurice said with a smile. "I should sit down I think, in case I fall." He uttered a cheery laugh as he perched on the edge of a huge tub chair in the corner of the cubicle and leaned back so his little old cock poked straight up to the ceiling. "I do so love the perks of my job." He smiled, grabbed Alec by the hair, and pushed his face into his crotch.

Alec took a deep breath and opened his mouth to receive him. The stubby legs shuddered as he took in the length. After a minute, Alec lost the initial repulsion and started to enjoy the odd little noises Maurice made when Alec did something right. Stroking his hand over the heavy ballsac, he smoothed, rubbed, jiggled, and squeezed. Alec realized he hadn't considered the men attached to the cocks he sucked at work or last night, as men, they were somehow intricately linked to Hamilton. Maurice had been different, to begin with at least. Maybe it was the doubt surrounding that damned leash. It didn't matter now, everything was back as it should be and sucking this little old guy was another way to make Hamilton happy. That, above all else, felt good. Just as Alec was really getting into it, the spray hit the back of his throat and it was all over. He sucked a little more and licked the cock before letting it slip out from his mouth.

"Such a wonderful boy." Maurice stroked his hair. "I do believe you enjoyed that."

"I did, sir. Thank you for letting me service you and for your help to my Master."

Master. Wherever the fuck that came from the first time he'd used it, it came from a different place now. It even sounded different, felt different in his mind and on his tongue. It felt comfortable. It just felt right.

Alec jumped as Hamilton spoke. "May we avail ourselves of your facilities? I believe my boy needs a good fucking to show how much his effort is appreciated."

"Of course. Here or a more private room?"

"Here is fine. Alec strip. Would you care to stay and watch, Maurice?"

"I would be delighted. Such a lovely boy."

Alec undressed and stood naked, waiting for instruction. Hamilton removed his pants and sat in the chair. He waved Alec over and ordered him to turn and bend over. Alec whimpered as Hamilton removed the butt plug. Slick fingers pushed extra lube into his well-worn ass.

"Sit on me, boy. I want you to fuck yourself on me." Alec started to sit astride face to face and smiling at being able to see Hamilton enjoy his ass. "No. Turn around. I want Maurice to see your face when you come."

Alec tried to hide the disappointment but Hamilton chuckled and slapped his thigh hard when he turned. Alec's passage was so raw from the plug he breathed in sharply when Hamilton's cock slid in to the hilt in one move. He let it settle into place and after another hard slap started to move. Within moments, Alec was rambling incoherently, soft mumbled words. "Master... thank you... good... love..." *Love?* "Love your cock, Master," he mumbled. "Only your cock for me."

Hamilton stroked his back, pulled his hair, reached around and pinched his nipples, all to the sound of his babbling until Hamilton held his hips fast and thrust up once, twice, and shot his load. Alec savored the feeling of being filled, Hamilton's mark inside as well as out.

"Stand." Alec's body mourned the loss of Hamilton's cock. Hamilton stood behind him and stroked his back with one hand and his chest with the other. He pushed a couple of fingers into Alec's sore ass and massaged his sweet spot. "Show Maurice what a good boy you are. Come for me, Alec." Alec cried out as without even a touch to his cock he spurted strings of pearly liquid into the air.

"Oh, bravo," clapped Maurice. "Such a beautiful boy. The best I've seen."

"And all mine, Maurice." Hamilton hugged Alec close, laughing at the smear of cum across his shirt when he finally let go.

The bell over the shop door rang to announce a new visitor. Alec's eyes widened. He'd completely forgotten he was in public. Sucking cocks, fucking, and anyone could have walked in.

"I'll see to that." Maurice stroked Alec's face. "Wonderful boy."

"I'll need to borrow one of your new shirts, Alec." Hamilton pulled on his pants and zipped himself up. "But first, I'd like you to come with me." He took Alec's hand.

"But—"

"Is there a problem?"

"Shouldn't I dress first?"

"No."

"There are people in the front."

"Are you questioning me, Alec?"

"No, Master. I'm sorry." Naked, in a kinky accessories store, on a Saturday afternoon, just around the corner from fucking Oxford Street with a trail of cum over his belly. *Jeez, I can't believe it!.*

Alec followed Hamilton onto the store's main area. Two men and a woman paused for no more than a moment to take in Alec's state of undress before continuing to browse. The woman clicked her fingers as she walked and the men huddled close behind her.

"Maurice I want to try this with Alec, is that okay?" Alec swallowed as he saw the butt plug Hamilton was holding. Twice the size of the small finger width one he'd been wearing and bigger than any they'd used so far for sex. *And* Alec's ass was raw already.

"Of course, sir. Please place it in the yellow bucket if you don't wish to purchase it."

"Alec, turn around and bend over."

He bit his tongue rather than double-check and obeyed. His face burned as he leaned against his knees with his legs spread. The weight of the collar fell forward. A reminder of why he was complying without hesitation.

"Pull your cheeks apart." He could feel the eyes of the other shoppers burning into his back as Hamilton pushed at his entrance with the plug. He winced a little. "Do you want more lube, Alec?"

"Yes please, Master."

Hamilton stepped away for a moment, leaving Alec wide open to the world. The bell over the door rang again, muffled voices entering. "Oh, fuck me, what a site. Maurice you will sell three times as much if that's on offer when people walk in and already prepped too."

"And spoken for." Hamilton's voice was cold as ice and hard as steel.

"My apologies."

"Good boy, Alec. It's okay." Hamilton stroked his back until his body stopped trembling. His breath settled and Hamilton started to probe his ass with the butt plug. "This is for home, Alec. You won't

112

have to wear this one out." With it fully inserted, he stroked Alec's back again. "Very good boy. Stand and face me."

It was easier than he thought it would be. Everything but Hamilton's blissful smile faded from view. Hamilton stroked his hair out of his face and whispered in his ear, kissed his lips so gently. Alec knew he was rock-hard in front of all those people, five at least now, maybe more. It mattered, but it didn't matter as long as Hamilton was there.

"How does it feel?"

"Sorry?"

"The plug, Alec. If you've forgotten you're wearing it already, we need a bigger one." Hamilton smoothed his cheek and Alec leaned automatically into that hand. It was such a special touch.

"I feel it, Master. It feels good when you... touch me."

"Good boy. I'll take that one Maurice. He'll keep it in for the journey home." Hamilton moved in and Alec's lips opened with a soft gasp at the kiss. "Very good, Alec. Go and get dressed. I'll be in shortly for a shirt."

Alec could hear the others chattering behind him. A man asked if Alec was for sale. *For sale?* Hamilton mentioned puppies at home, the man was welcome to visit, but Alec was not available for play. *Until tonight of course when he would suck cocks in a sex club for practice.* But Hamilton didn't mention that. Alec made a mental note to ask about puppies, which he figured related to the boys. The new possessiveness in Hamilton's voice made Alec feel good. Maybe it had always been there, but Alec felt as though something had changed. Maybe it was the wristbands. Maybe that was why Dylan was so peaceful.

A month ago, Alec had been a virgin. Now he had a plug up his ass, had sucked off an old man and put on a sex show in a shop, not to mention the countless number of cocks he'd sucked. The smile which spread over his face came as no surprise. The reality made Alec feel sexy. Sexier than his new clothes or the new haircut Hamilton had squeezed from a celebrity stylist without an appointment. Sexiness oozed from his pores and he loved it. Jules would have to look out—Alec was hot on his tail.

His cock protested at the tightness of his jeans and his ass ached. There was no way he'd be sitting down on the Underground for the ride home. He paused to look at the gold bracelets on his wrists. The links packed tightly together like a watchstrap without the face. The matching choker around his throat was visible over his t-shirt. Another smile as he fingered it.

"I have the leash." Alec jumped. Hamilton was running it through his hands. "I think you like the feel of that chain."

"I do. Very much."

"Do you know what it means?"

"Yes, Master."

"Tell me."

"It means I belong to you."

"That's right. But not just that, Alec, it means it's my duty to take care of you."

Alec took the few steps to stand in front of Hamilton. He took his hand with the leash still in it, which didn't seem so scary anymore, and raised it to his lips to kiss. "Thank you, Master."

"You make me very happy, Alec."

"I want to make you happy, Master. I will follow your instruction and act on your requests always."

"Always?"

"Always."

"And if I tell you to go into the store and suck every cock there?"

"I will do it, for you." And he would, Alec knew he would, without question. Every single one would make him happy regardless of the man attached to it or the reasons behind it, as long as it was at Hamilton's request.

"Good boy. But we don't have time for that now. I have to get home to my puppies. They'll be tearing the place up."

"Puppies? That's the boys, right?"

"Yes, Alec. A concept you'll understand in time. Just know you're not one."

The thought comforted him. Alec knew how much Hamilton cared for the boys and yet he was different. Perhaps not more, not yet, but special in a way he was beginning to catch glimpses. Alec was almost disappointed he wouldn't have the chance to show Hamilton he meant what he'd said about dishing out blowjobs in the shop. He gathered his bags and followed Hamilton from the store, feeling every step vibrating through his cock with the jolt of the plug in his ass. It was a double-edged sword of torture and ecstasy and he loved it. Loved that it was their secret—walking the streets of London with his lover's touch firmly planted inside him.

The Club

The puppies had indeed torn the place apart. Piles of DVDs lay strewn over the floor with food crumbs and wrappers in between, and Sebastian had a long red scratch mark over his shoulder. Hamilton sighed and the three of them fell at his feet, foreheads pressed to the floor.

"I'm going to have to punish them, Alec. You may not like this. It's very different watching rather than receiving."

"Would you like me to wait in your room, Master?"

"No. It's good that you witness it as a reminder."

The three naked boys shivered together. Alec smiled to himself. Whatever was going to happen it looked very much like they'd planned it.

"Sebastian, who scratched you?"

"Dylan, Master. It was an accident. He tried to catch me as I slipped off the bed."

"What were you doing that you almost fell off the bed?"

"He was tickling me, Master."

"Dylan, get the long paddle."

Dylan stomped out of the room with a face like thunder. It was the first time Alec had seen him react in such a way to something Hamilton had asked of him. He returned moments later with a half inch piece of wood, four inches wide and about eighteen inches long. The end curved to twice the width of the handle, which looked like it had a padded grip. Alec was pretty sure it wasn't the one Hamilton used on him. It seemed too big. This one would definitely swat both ass cheeks at the same time. Dylan fell back to his knees and raised his hands over his head to raise the paddle aloft.

Hamilton took the paddle from Dylan, and in the split-second of doing so he changed. He grabbed Dylan by the upper arm and dragged him across the room as the boy yelped. "Over the stool," he roared. Dylan almost tripped over himself but there was no anger in Hamilton just an overwhelming presence. There was no mercy either. Dylan jumped as the paddle swiped his bare ass. "Why am I punishing you, Dylan?"

"I have not respected... your wishes... or your home... in your absence, Master." The swats increased in intensity and Dylan let out a strangled cry.

"And your penalty?"

"My attitude... at your request... for the long paddle. Master, please... I'm sorry... I was bad."

The exchange petered out but the blows continued. Alec had the feeling this form of punishment was not in Dylan's plan at all and he wondered what other forms of correction Hamilton used which Dylan had hoped for. Over and over, the paddle hit true until Dylan's ass was as red as a beetroot. He'd stopped crying out with the blows and Alec caught the subtle change in his posture. After three further slaps, Hamilton stopped. He placed the paddle on the table. "Dylan, you may stand."

His legs were a little shaky but he wasn't trembling as he'd been at the beginning.

"Do you have anything you wish to say?"

Dylan kept his head bowed. "Thank you, Master for caring about my behavior enough to correct me." A shuddery breath ran through his chest. "I really am sorry. I won't mess up your things again or play silly games that can cause people harm."

"Very well. Stand and watch the remaining punishments and consider your actions. I will decide at the end if I am satisfied."

"Thank you, Master."

Wow, it was a much more serious deal than Alec had received yesterday. But Dylan seemed well versed in the process. Alec hoped he wouldn't need more training in this particular department.

"Brendon, heel." The boy scurried to his Master with his head bowed low. "Take your position." The scene played out much the same, with a similar exchange and Hamilton dealing out the same blows across Brendon's ass. Alec didn't count them but there seemed less. Brendon was louder, however, and his ass no less red by the end. Brendon stood next to Dylan.

Sebastian was up next. His punishment was definitely lighter. Though again, his ass just as ruddy when it was finished. "Due to the severity of your actions further punishment will be required. I have never seen this place in such a mess and all in a few hours. Accompanied by games that endanger your well-being in my absence, a firmer message is required to ensure that you do not repeat this behavior. Do you understand?"

They answered in unison, heads still bowed. "Yes, Master."

"Alec will plug each one of you. You will accompany us to the club and spend the evening in cages." Brendon and Dylan gasped. Sebastian started to tremble. "You will not abuse my trust again."

A chorus of "no, Master" followed.

Each boy leaned over a stool and Alec went to work with the plugs. He fitted Brendon's plug, bigger than his own and moved on to Dylan. It was the same size as Brendon's but Dylan was tighter, there was more resistance and it took a little patience and a lot of lube. Alec was surprised to see the plug Hamilton passed him for Sebastian was bigger than the other two. It took even more work and a lot of patience to get it fully inserted.

Leaving the boys on their knees, with the order to continue considering the consequences of their actions, Hamilton took Alec through to the bedroom and removed his plug. He took his time, licking and fingering Alec's stretched hole, before turning him over and sucking in the length of his cock. Alec's body shuddered with restraint. Hamilton smiled. He let the cock slip from his lips. "Come for me, Alec." The release was immediate. Hamilton caught most of it in his mouth, tongue hanging out to lap at the air. The rest he rubbed into his face. "I like wearing you on me."

That was hot. Alec shivered with pleasure at the thought of Hamilton being out in public with his cum marking him. Was it different to the way he acted with the other boys? No. Hamilton often had the boys come over his hand or chest. Alec would have to try it, see if the effect was different when it was conscious. Right now, he was curious about the rest of the evening.

"Master, why is Sebastian wearing a bigger plug?"

"Ah, yes. The cages are fuck cages. They restrain the body with the ass butting through the end of the cage in a perfect position for penetration. The cages are set on a podium next to my tables for anyone, and I mean anyone, to use when we are there. Sebastian needs more time to open up and accommodate extending fucking. The larger plug will make him more pliable."

"But they do like it don't they?"

"Yes, normally they do. But they don't like the cages on a Saturday night and they each have sore ass cheeks. Think how tender you still are after yesterday and imagine being poked and prodded all evening. They'll have trouble walking tomorrow. But they *will* think twice before misbehaving again."

"How many?"

Hamilton shrugged. "Maybe twenty each. Often the men that utilize cage-fucks aren't looking to climax. They want to *mark* as many asses during the evening as they can so they thrust into each for no more than a few minutes at a time. Some look out for particular boys they like and do have a full fuck, but it can cause problems with other guests if they monopolize a caged boy for too long. There are other boys available for longer fucks. It does mean that the numbers can get pretty high when it's busy. They use a marker pen to register numbers. Tops mark their thigh, and the bottom's ass on penetration."

"Is that why they get sore, because of so many men?"

"No, it's not the numbers. It's the length of time in one position and being fucked continuously. Different sized cocks too, I guess, and some of the men can be a little rough with their thrusting."

Hamilton reached into one of the bags from their shopping expedition. "I bought you these." The tiniest white rubber shorts emerged. "The color denotes your ass is mine." He also pulled out a pair of black kneepads. "You will thank me for these by the time you are through with this evening." Alec took them and squeezed the spongy material. "Now there are rules in the club," Hamilton continued. "No bodily fluids. You will suck every cock I send to you but they will wear a condom. My priority is to keep you safe. It will mean you have to work harder. You may stop only to drink the water I provide for you. You will speak to no one even if they speak to you. Do you understand?"

"Yes, Master."

"A little powder will help you slide into the shorts. It's in the bathroom cabinet. Nothing underneath."

It wasn't until Alec picked them up that he realized they were spilt at the back. "Master, they are—"

"Supposed to be like that. How else will I fuck you?"

"Oh, I see."

"Is that a problem?"

120

Alec held them higher to look closer, wondering whether they'd cover his ass or gape open. "No, Master. No problem at all."

"Good, get dressed."

Alec felt naked as he left his clothes in the changing room at the door of the club. The rubber pants were so small and so tight, they gapped at the back and his balls hung out at the front. There was a zipper at the front that opened from the bottom up just enough that Hamilton could show off Alec's cock should he choose to. But he fared better than the other boys. They were naked except for their silver collars and bracelets. They walked head down as Hamilton led them through the main club arena and up a sweeping staircase.

It was quieter upstairs. The deep red décor added to the ambience of sultriness. Hamilton was right about it being busy and Alec's eyes were drawn to every corner where it seemed some kind of sex act was going on. A month ago, he would have said the club was someone's fantasy had he been told about it, now it seemed an extension of his everyday life. He was sure, though, that not all of the people there indulged themselves in such a way outside of the club. Some of them had to be sightseers.

They arrived at a small grouping of tables and a long, low platform on which stood the cages. Sebastian threw himself at Hamilton's feet. "Please, Master. I'm so sorry. I'll never misbehave again. Anything but the cage, Master, please."

"You will accept your punishment, Sebastian, and refrain from this behavior immediately."

Sebastian placed his hands against Hamilton's thighs and kissed his cock through his pants. Big, sad eyes pleaded but Hamilton strapped him in a cage along with the other two. He removed the plugs. If Sebastian's cage hadn't held him in place, he would have collapsed. As it was, the cage held him in the perfect pose for fucking.

There was a part of Alec that wanted to tear the cage apart and hold Sebastian close to stop the trembles which shook his body. But it was out of his hands. He had yet to be inducted into the strange rules of puppies and their Masters. Maybe he never would be.

"Ah, Hamilton's beautiful boys." A stranger stroked Dylan's rump and slapped it. Alec winced with him. That would have stung like hell. "Are they open?"

"They are indeed." Hamilton stepped back and watched as the man lifted his shirt to reveal an already impressive erection. He slipped on a condom, a little lube and one thrust later, was buried to the hilt in Dylan's body. Alec's cock jumped to attention. Hamilton settled into one of the deep leather chairs next to the cages. A tray of drinks had already been delivered by a waiter wearing a scrap of fabric as a loincloth that left nothing to the imagination. "On your knees, Alec. Here, in front of me."

Alec obeyed. Hamilton stroked his hair and watched as the three boys were fucked. Just as the first man was finishing in Dylan, Alec became aware of someone standing in front of him. He looked up to see an attractive face, good body, in his early forties at a guess. A faint memory stirred, but Alec couldn't pin it down.

"Is your boy available?"

"Mouth only." The man with his faintly familiar face nodded and opened his fly. He was already hard and didn't have to be asked, he rolled on a condom and pushed his cock against Alec's lips. Alec turned to Hamilton who nodded and Alec opened his mouth. Everything he'd experienced so far failed to prepare him for what happened next. The man grabbed his hair and rammed the full length of his cock down Alec's throat. He panicked, grasped at thin air to pull away and tried desperately to remove the intrusion so he could breathe. A moment later he was free, sitting back on his feet with Hamilton's arms around him. The man was gone. "I'm sorry, darling. Don't worry. I'll make sure they don't do that again. Are you okay?"

"Yes, Master. Sorry. I still find that difficult. I'll do better next time."

"That's a good boy. It's just practice."

"Yes, Master, so I can be better for you."

"My beautiful boy."

A couple of hours later Alec was really getting the hang of it. He'd lost count of the number of cocks sucked and his jaw ached, but he felt as though he'd achieved something. Not as many as had fucked the boys that was for sure. Sebastian was mewling with each new partner and his body tensed with every thrust.

"It's time to go, boys. Sebastian has had enough. Finish up and we'll head home. Alec spread your legs and move around so I can fuck you."

Alec smiled at the man whose cock he removed from his mouth so he could bend and shuffle to accommodate Hamilton. Then sucked it back in. The first thrust into his body synchronized with the thrust into his throat and he felt skewered. It pushed the cock further in than usual but this time the intrusion was comfortable. He swallowed it down and the man came immediately. Alec felt his jizz pumping into the condom. As the man pulled out he stroked Alec's hair and face as he watched Hamilton fuck Alec ruthlessly. Alec wanted it so much, pushed back into those thrusts and reached back to grasp hold of Hamilton's hips. He was shocked to hear his own voice begging for more, harder faster. *Please, Master, please.* Sebastian—freed from his cage now—crawled between Alec's legs and sucked down his cock. Alec couldn't think, an emptiness rolled around his brain until he heard Hamilton's voice.

"Come for me, Alec. Feed Sebastian and take me with you." The orgasm, unleashed through Alec's body, pumped into Sebastian's throat. He felt Hamilton's own liquid shoot into him, adding to the slipperiness. Hamilton pulled him back to sit against him. "Good boy, Alec. Let Dylan and Brendan clean you up." Alec leaned forward on all fours and the boys licked his ass clean of Hamilton's cum. It was soothing and torturing at the same time over his sensitive hole.

The man he'd just sucked before was still watching. "How much for the boy?" he said in a peremptory tone

"Alec is not for sale."

"Just a few hours."

"Alec is not a whore you can purchase for entertainment." Hamilton's voice expressed his impatience and verged on angry. "In using his mouth this evening you have had a rare privilege. Be grateful for it and leave us in peace."

Alec was aware of security moving in around their little enclosure. He wondered if they were the reason his first disaster had disappeared without a trace. They certainly looked ready to pounce on the guy in front of him now.

"Alec, don't you remember me?"

Alec looked first at Hamilton with a questioning frown and then up at the man. And it clicked. His eyes widened. "Mr. Wilson? I... I didn't recognize you."

"It's okay, Alec. I just wanted to make sure you're okay."

Hamilton sounded pissed at the guy. "You ask that *after* he sucked your cock, I notice. Not before."

"That's true. I have my guilty pleasures. Alec was my star pupil. While it was a surprise to watch him suck cock all evening, it was also an opportunity too good to pass up. I just thought if his services were for sale..."

"They're not."

Mr. Wilson sighed. He looked down at Alec as if searching him for something. "Alec, is this what you want?"

"Yes, Mr. Wilson. Master, takes very good care of me."

"So it seems."

"I wanted to practice. To be better for him. This was my choice."

"I see. But he fucks you in public."

"Yes."

"And you're okay with that?"

Alec felt his own patience fraying. "Yes I am."

The other boys draped themselves leisurely over Hamilton and Alec. Together they presented a united front.

"And I won't find you in a cage next week?"

"Not that it's any of your business, but Alec is *not* a puppy," Hamilton snapped. "He's my lover. My partner. If you do not understand this lifestyle, *Mister* Wilson, I suggest you find yourself another club."

"Thank you, Mr. Hamilton. You didn't need to give me an explanation, but I'm grateful for it. I've made use of yours boys before and they have always appeared well cared for and happy. It was just a shock to see Alec among them."

After a moment's consideration, Hamilton relented a bit. "You obviously care for Alec, even if you do want to fuck him."

"Actually, I would have just made sure he was happy. A blowjob is one thing. I wouldn't fuck a former student."

Alec doubted that was true. Lack of opportunity more like. Now he thought about it, the guy had always been a bit odd.

Hamilton had his thinking face on. "And what do you teach?"

"Maths. Thank you again for your time."

Hamilton handed Wilson a card. "You can call to see Alec as long as you are in my presence at all times. You should see for yourself that he is happy at home as well as here."

"Thank you."

Back at the apartment, Hamilton ran a bath and bathed the boys. He spent extra time with Sebastian to massage his arms and legs for a little longer. Twenty-five men had placed a pen mark on his ass to show they'd fucked him. Dylan had thirty and Brendan twenty-four. Hamilton rubbed salve into their overused holes and kissed them all good night before tucking them into bed. He was tired by the time he ran a bath for Alec. They soaked together and cuddled and caressed. It had been little over a month and yet Alec couldn't remember the time before him.

"At work on Monday, Alec, you must treat me as you would normally. People will notice those wristbands. It's up to you to convince everyone they're a fashion choice. Apart from the other office boys, no one can know about this. Even they will never know the extent of it."

"Yes, Master."

"I've told you, you may call me Rick, when we relax together."

Alec snuggled back against his chest. "Thank you. Rick. I think… it's soon I know, but I think I'm falling in love with you. Is that okay?" Alec turned to look into Hamilton's face.

"That's very okay." He smiled one of his blindingly beautiful smiles. "I've loved you from the moment I saw you splutter as I sucked your cock for the first time." They chuckled together. "I've never felt like this, Alec. It's why I can't share you. I won't. I'm sorry that I can't be just for you."

"It's okay, Rick. You'll never lie to me. You fuck other people, I fuck other people. But we are only for each other. I like that it's just you inside me, and I like that it's without a barrier between us. I don't want you to change for me. I will love *you*, as you are. Not who I want you to be."

"Thank you." Hamilton brushed over Alec's lips with a soft kiss. "Alec, that man, Mr. Wilson. Did you have a crush on him?"

126

"Not at all. He was just a maths teacher. I didn't even recognize him until he made a fuss about my knowing him—that I should remember him."

"I'd like to let him come to the apartment so that you can suck his cock again, maybe let him play with you a little."

"If that's what you want, Rick, of course." Alec felt there was more to Hamilton's statement, but he didn't seem ready to share it. It wasn't a problem, Alec trusted that Hamilton would tell him what he needed to know, when he needed to know it. *If,* he needed to know at all.

They were soon dried and settled into bed. Hamilton held him tightly as if he might float away. "My Alec and his maths teacher. It conjures interesting pictures in my head."

"I am your Alec. And you can conjure any image you want for me. I will do it."

"I know you will. Now sleep. Tomorrow the boys will need to be pampered again and packed off home."

"Will you send me home?"

"Only if you want to go. This is your home now, Alec. Anything I have is yours, the boys included. We'll work out the details as time passes but for me it's very simple. You're mine and I love you."

Alec settled into the deepest sleep since childhood, safe in the arms of his first love.

Sebastian

Alec awoke in the night to see Sebastian stood by the bed shivering. Hamilton, still asleep at his side, didn't stir as Alec lifted the covers and Sebastian climbed into bed and snuggled into Alec's side. "Thank you, Alec."

"Are you okay?"

Sebastian peered over Alec's shoulder to check on Hamilton and settled when a faint snore resounded from Hamilton's direction. "The other boys were teasing me again. They say Master babies me, that I can't take what they can. I'm scared Alec."

"Of what?"

"What if Master sells me because I'm no good. Because he has you."

"I can't promise he won't, Sebastian, because I don't know how these things work." Alec didn't see how anyone *could* be sold, even in the cock-eyed circles in which they seemed to socialize. "But I know it won't be because of me," he added.

"You're always so kind to me. I like you, Alec. A lot."

"Get some sleep." There was no denying Alec had the urge to protect Sebastian, care for, and keep him safe. His little quirks and wistful sighs always made Alec smile, and hell, did they have chemistry. Sebastian made Alec's blood run hot with just a trace of fingers over his skin. Almost as much as Hamilton, but not quite the same.

Alec wrapped Sebastian in his arms, feeling his body warm against his own, and wondered if he should raise the subject with Hamilton in the morning. If Sebastian was scared, perhaps Alec should be more concerned about what was really going on. He'd always assumed the boys were there of their own free will rather than slaves or property in the literal sense. The thought sat uncomfortably in his stomach, especially after tonight and Sebastian begging not to be put in the cage. Had he really been fucked by twenty guys against his will? It couldn't be. Hamilton wouldn't.

A soft contented snore slipped from Sebastian's lips. Alec chuckled and kissed the boy's cheek. Whatever's going on, he thought, you don't sleep like that if you're deeply troubled.

Alec felt the subtle grinding of hips against his ass, the tender stroke of Hamilton's fingers over his thigh, and hot lips against the nape of his neck. "Thank you," Hamilton whispered. "He's a sensitive boy. It's good that he can relate to you."

"You don't mind?"

"Sebastian is very special to me. In a different way to you. Maybe one day he'll tell you his story. I've worried about his detachment from the other boys, that his life was harder than it should be living with them, but he's happier with you around."

"Do you own him?"

Alec felt Hamilton slip his growing erection between his cheeks. "Only as much as his mind allows me to. He's free to make his own choices, if that's what you're asking. Our bond as master and slave is no more than a consensual agreement for a certain relationship dynamic."

"So you wouldn't sell him?"

"I could no more sell him, than I could you or an employee at the office. But the idea, the possibility, is part of what makes the relationship work for them—it makes it real on a different level."

His breathing was coming faster and Hamilton's cockhead nudged against Alec's hole. He was tender from so much plug wearing but he still wanted that cock. His own erection butted against Sebastian's hip as he slept on, oblivious. Alec heard the cap of the lube bottle pop open and a moment later slick fingers slipped inside.

"Don't think about it now, Alec." Hamilton's whisper turned into nibbling around Alec's ear. "Think about me." A slow, sensual, penetration to the hilt followed, filling Alec's heart and mind as well as his body. "I love you."

"I love you, Rick."

Hamilton pulled Alec back against his body and Sebastian rolled away still wrapped in his own dreams to give them space for their own dance of love.

Sundays were such wonderfully peaceful days. This one was particularly quiet with the boys and Alec nursing tender butts both from beatings and too much sex. But the mood was light and cheery and Alec stretched out on the sofa with Sebastian snuggled into his side. Hamilton played chess with Dylan, and Brendon fussed in the kitchen over the Sunday roast.

"Do you think Master will let me live with you, Alec, when we're not here?" Sebastian's voice was so quiet Alec wasn't sure he heard him correctly. "We get on well, don't we? Please say you want me." He clung, limpet-like, to Alec's chest.

"Sebastian, I can't make decisions like that."

"You can ask him. He'll give you anything you want."

"I don't know if that's true."

Sebastian's grip loosened. "It's okay. I know I'm a nuisance."

"That's not it at all. Crap! How do I explain this?"

"You don't have to. I get it." Sebastian started to sit up but Alec pulled him down into a fierce hug.

"No you don't. I care about you, Sebastian, want to look after you, but this is all so new to me. I can barely look after myself on the nights I'm not here."

"That's why you need me. We'll look after each other."

It was Alec holding on tight now. He didn't know what to say, just knew he wanted what Sebastian was offering. The nights at home alone were the worst thing about his life. It was hard to adjust to the silence, the lack of life around him. Sebastian had brought into focus a need Alec hadn't been aware of, a missing piece in the puzzle. But Alec's apartment was small, the second bedroom kitted out as an office. Even if he cleared it, only a single bed would fit in there. And Hamilton. Alec couldn't ask. It would be like asking permission to be unfaithful.

"Think about it." Sebastian kissed Alec's cheek and snuggled back into his chest.

Think about it? How the fuck was Alec supposed to think about anything else?

"Come on boys." Alec started at Hamilton's voice. "Brendon is serving lunch."

Lunch, cuddles, sex, and home. Home to an empty flat with only his own hand for company. But Hamilton had said he could stay tonight, that this was his home now. That certainly gave him the extra to think about that he needed. But both things slipped away when he caught sight of the leg of lamb Brendon was carving at the table, the tray piled high with roast potatoes, and the steaming dishes of vegetables. His stomach growled approvingly. He'd never eaten so well as in the hands of these boys. "Brendon, I think I want to marry you."

"That would make you the wife," Brendon said over the laughter from the others. "Looks like the dishes are your responsibility this afternoon, dear."

Alec was pleased, or rather relieved, to see that other than an initial wink and a cheeky grin, Tom was his usual self on Monday morning. He'd sorted things out with Emma, he told Alec. She wasn't cheating, it turned out, but had been considering breaking it off. After a nice long, girlie chat, as Tom called it, they'd found new ground to move forward together. "I wouldn't have been able to do it if it wasn't for you, Alec."

"Why, what did Alec do for you?" They both looked at Chloe and burst out laughing. "Fine, don't let me into your little boys' joke."

"Problem, Chloe?" Alec never tired of seeing that man smile. Hamilton leaned on the desk partition and into Chloe's line of sight.

"No, Mr. Hamilton, just catching up on weekend news." Hamilton appearing over her shoulder at inopportune moments never seemed to faze Chloe. She just breezed on through her day without a care. Tom on the other hand turned bright pink and started to shuffle papers.

"Alec, I'd like to speak to you for a moment."

"Certainly, Mr. Hamilton. I'll be right with you."

Alec watched Hamilton's ass as he walked away. Would he ever stop drooling over the sight of it?

"He's different," Chloe said. "Must have had a good weekend."

"Why do you say that?"

"I don't know. He just seems… mellow today."

"Plenty of good sex will do that to you," Tom said with a grin. Alec noted Tom seemed pretty mellow himself.

"You think he's having lots of good sex?" Alec asked, trying not to sound too pleased with himself.

"Sorry, sport," Chloe said. "That man looks dreamy-eyed. It's a nice change from the usual ass-whooping fire he has going on. You'll have to find yourself a new crush, Alec. The boss man is officially spoken for."

Well fuck. Alec was too stunned to break out into the victory dance his brain was doing. No, he had to be down to earth. His boss's mood was more likely down to a new fantasy Hamilton had playing out in his head than it was anything to do with Alec. "Well, best not keep him waiting. Even if he is in a good mood."

"Hello, beautiful," Hamilton smiled when Alec entered the office. "Lock the door and come here."

Definitely a good mood. And Hamilton sat on the sofa rather than behind his desk. That could mean heavy petting or serious chat. It still amazed Alec that nobody in the office ever cottoned on to his glazed and disheveled appearance whenever he left Hamilton's office. Admittedly, he was always careful to check in the mirror and straighten himself out as best he could but nevertheless it seemed denial was alive and well in the City of London.

Alec took a deep breath as Hamilton pulled him close and looked up into his face. Nimble fingers extracted Alec's swelling cock from his pants and Hamilton took a long slow lick up the shaft and around the tip. "My turn to service you for a change." There was mischief in Hamilton's eyes as he began work on Alec's member. He paused for a moment as though thinking. "Come when you're ready, Alec, as I usually do with you." And then he got back to the job in hand.

Free permission to come when ready. Fuck. Did Alec even know how anymore? It seemed he did. Hamilton had skills that Alec still needed to learn despite the stint on his knees at the club and the last month of cock sucking. It didn't take long for Alec to lose all reason and fall over the edge of the precipice he was so used to teetering on for most of the day.

Hamilton licked his lips and tucked Alec away. He wrapped his arms around Alec's hips and nestled against his crotch. "Thank you, I enjoyed that."

Alec fingered Hamilton's hair. It was growing more blond from the sun and slightly longer than he usually wore it. "I did too, thank you. It was unexpected."

"I do hope to keep you on your toes." He straightened up and patted the seat directly next to him. "Sit with me. I need to speak to you."

Alec shuffled closer. "Is everything okay?"

"Perfect, really, you've nothing to be concerned about." Alec sat sideways on the sofa, with his knee on the seat so he could face Hamilton. Hamilton took his hand and started to play with his fingers. It was very distracting. "Firstly, I wanted to talk to you about discipline. You've had first-hand experience of it but I should apologize for Friday."

"I understand why it was needed."

"That's not the point. I shouldn't have carried out that kind of punishment without discussing it with you first, without setting boundaries, making sure you knew what the consequences of breaking the rules were and most importantly negotiating those rules in the first place."

"I didn't realize it was so complicated."

"It isn't. It's very straightforward. The problem is you've taken to this life so easily I forget we've missed some of the basic steps."

"Okay, what do I need to know?"

Hamilton explained the ins and outs of master/slave boundaries and what he felt were acceptable boundaries for their particular relationship. He gave hints at how it differed to the arrangement he had with the houseboys.

"Aside from the main difference I have to consider the way I deal with indiscretions at work. It should be different from those at home. I didn't make that distinction on Friday when I plied your ass with the paddle. I would never use physical punishment on an office boy."

"Then why do you have a paddle in the office?"

Hamilton grinned. "Because some of our clients like to role-play."

"They do?"

"Don't worry, we have boys specifically trained in those areas. Just know it isn't for punishment, it's for play."

"What else have you got hiding in there?"

"You're getting off track, Alec."

Alec choked back an inappropriate chuckle. "Sorry. But you know, I would prefer if there wasn't one set of rules for home and one for the office. If I step out of line I need the punishment to be the same across the board, even if you do wait until we're at home to deliver it."

"That is something I appreciate very much. I find it very difficult to think of you as an office boy. From that first weekend you were mine, not part of the Order, and now you wear my bands—"

"The Order?" The second he blurted out the words Alec regretted his rude interruption. Fortunately, Hamilton seemed to take no notice.

"The club I refer to—the inner organization that we work for within this company—is officially known as the Order of Gentleman. You'll often hear members refer to it as the Order or GC."

"Has it been around long?"

"Hundreds of years and its reach is worldwide."

Alec let this surprising fact sink in for a moment. "Are there meetings and, I don't know, a clubhouse or something?"

Hamilton rolled his eyes and smiled. "We aren't Masons, Alec. Though some of the Order are. Our influence is mostly through business although there are some aspects of it that are more personal."

"Such as?"

"You will always receive help if you need it, in any form. We look after our own. You'll understand more of what I mean as you attend official functions. At the moment you are a member of the Order as a Trainee in Service."

"And what are you?"

"I'm a fully inducted member and Officer or as we more commonly say these days, Manager of Service. When your training is complete you will be a Member In Service and given a grade so that other members know what to expect of you."

It seemed straightforward enough, even if a little archaic. "What are the options?"

"You'll be first level, offering oral services alongside your general duties. Second level is full sex. Various other levels cover speciality services such as role-play, pain play, and domination. Unless you're one day considered as a Service Manager you really don't have to worry about what those levels entail."

"I'm pretty low on the ladder then really."

"Don't think of it that way. Your level of attainment within the Order is not based on your performance in bed, Alec. It's determined by how you handle yourself within the organization and conduct the real business of investments and advice."

"Like the accounts I gained from the lunch meeting?"

"Yes. Your service status gave you access to some important clients it would have taken another five years for you to gain within the conventional office structure. But you will only keep those clients if you perform well with their investments and not because you swallow their cock or have a pretty face. In the same way, letting them fuck you isn't going to keep an account if you've lost them money or given bad advice."

"Can I suck your cock, right now, I mean?"

"You want to?"

"I always want to."

"You drive me crazy, Alec, I just love the way you think." Hamilton unzipped his pants and leaned back on the sofa. It was more of a leisurely worshiping than a hot blowjob but Alec still received his reward, the flow of warm liquid over his tonsils. Hamilton's voice was husky when he spoke again. "You are definitely getting better at that."

"I like to please you, Master."

"Oh god, that reminds me," Hamilton spluttered. Alec tucked away his favorite cock and crawled up for a kiss. "Stop distracting me. We have other things to discuss." But he found it hard to suppress a smile and a low chuckle.

"But I like kissing you."

Hamilton surrendered and let their lips mesh and tongues tangle. Alec started to grind his hips against Hamilton's thigh, but he called a halt. "You're creasing my suit. You can get away with the odd wrinkle, I can't. Back to business." Alec sat back with a humph and a pout that had Hamilton reaching to brush a thumb over his bottom lip. "Cheer up, sweetness, you're going to like this."

"I'm listening."

"I'd like you consider having Sebastian come to live with you."

"You're kidding?"

"I thought you got on well with him."

"I do, I mean it would be great but…" *But what?* Alec wanted Sebastian to be at home so what was the problem?

"He's not happy living with Brendon and Dylan and to be honest since you've been with us the relationship between the boys seems strained. I'd like him to have a little space from them. I don't think they mean to close ranks on him during the week but they're very into each other when I'm not around. Sebastian feels like a spare part over there."

"He asked you?"

"Don't be angry with him. I thought you'd like the idea. It never crossed my mind it would be a problem."

"It isn't."

"But?"

"What happens to my weeknights with you?"

"Nothing changes between us, Alec. It just means Sebastian will look after that tip you call an apartment. He's very house-proud you know."

"I only have one bedroom."

"Are you honestly telling me you'd be sleeping in separate beds if you had two bedrooms?"

Alec pondered the statement for a moment. "So we can have sex, on our own?"

Hamilton tugged at Alec's arm and cuddled him onto his chest. "When the boys are away from me they please themselves. I know you haven't had that luxury yet, but you should have. I fuck whoever I want, whenever I want. You should at least be able to make those decisions when you're not in my company."

"But what about permission to come?"

"On evenings when we're not getting together you are free from the time you leave the office until you return the next morning."

The new plan looked good. In fact, it looked very good. The idea of being able to fuck Sebastian whenever he wanted, get each other off in their own home for their own pleasure.

"And we'd both still be your boys?"

"You'll always be my boys, even when you leave me."

"I'll never leave you."

Hamilton kissed his hair and stroked his arm. "Actually, there is something else I'd like you to consider." Alec held tight to Hamilton's chest. Surely he wouldn't move him on, he couldn't, Alec wouldn't go. "I'd like you to take Sebastian as *your* boy."

Alec sat up straight and blinked a few times. "I don't understand."

"I'd like to think that you have more potential within the Order then the average office boy. The sooner you have experience of managing a boy of your own the quicker things will happen for you.

Sebastian is very fond of you, Alec. He'll settle quickly and is very well behaved but he also has the strength to guide you in his care to ensure his own happiness without being difficult."

"You want me to have my own houseboy?"

"Is that so shocking?"

There were no thoughts in Alec's head. He searched for words, but there was just nothing—empty.

"Why don't you go back to work and think it over. I'll talk to you again over lunch." Hamilton met his lips in a brief kiss and made his way back to his desk. "One o'clock for lunch. I'd like to eat out today."

Alec nodded and left Hamilton to his work. The world still felt unhooked and shaky when he found his own desk and he couldn't seem to tune into it as it swirled around him. His own houseboy. Sebastian his, actually his, with all that entailed—caring for him, making him happy, choosing his lovers, bringing him to climax and holding him afterward. And Sebastian had asked to leave Hamilton—wanted to leave his master, a man he loved more than anything—to be with Alec.

Alec wanted to cry. He didn't know if it was from happiness or because he was scared. How was he supposed to look after someone else the way Hamilton did? He wouldn't know what Sebastian needed. But Hamilton said Sebastian would guide him, and hadn't Sebastian said he would look after Alec as well, that they'd look after each other? If Alec was going to have to learn to manage for the Order, Sebastian was the best support system he could hope for because Alec knew that Sebastian would make sure he got it right.

Fucking hell. From virgin to office boy to houseboy to Master. Alec had definitely found the fast-track to something. For the moment, he'd didn't want to think about where the path was leading him.

The Handover

The week had passed so fast Alec hadn't had time to breathe let alone think about what the weekend would bring. Details for the new projects he'd gained at the Service lunch had been arriving and there was a lot of preparation involved to establish the correct files and routines for ensuring the relevant deadlines were met. It was the first real kick in his work load other than sex since taking on the role as office boy. He liked it. It was safe to say, he really liked it. Even better was the new easiness and camaraderie with Tom. He should have given his friend a blowjob years ago.

But now it was Friday again and tonight was the big announcement. Sebastian already knew what was happening although he hadn't spoken to Alec about it directly. This weekend he would officially move in with Alec and tonight they were to have a handover party and break the news to Brendon and Dylan. Alec guessed they'd be over the moon: more room at the apartment and they'd get to be alone during the week for all their lovey-dovey stuff. But at the same time a sense of pressure built in Alec's chest and he wasn't sure of the reason.

He tidied his desk for the weekend. The office was unusually quiet. Alec had either stayed later than intended or everyone had gone early. He locked his filing cabinet and turned to find Tom leaning on the partition.

"Hey, you." He grinned at Alec in a hopeful way.

"Don't tell me. You're after your Friday blowjob."

Tom flushed and looked around the office quickly. "Don't say it out loud."

"Anyone who heard would think I was joking. Now what is it?"

"I was wondering if you had a bit of time, perhaps we could go for a drink."

"You *do* want a blowjob." Alec snickered. "I knew you wouldn't be able to resist my charms."

"Alec, I want to ask you a favor."

"You don't have to pepper me up with beer for that. Just ask me." Tom came around the desk and stepped in close to Alec. He stroked a hand over his cheek and reached for his hand. "Oh, god, you're going to ask me to marry you."

"Shut up, stupid. I've been thinking about last week. About what you did. I… Fuck, I didn't think this would be so difficult."

Alec slipped a hand around the back of Tom's neck and pulled him in for a kiss. It was tentative at first, but Tom relaxed into it, pushed his tongue into Alec's mouth and let Alec slip an arm around his waist. Their hips met and Alec felt Tom's erection but didn't pull away, just let it run its course. "Now ask me," he said, bumping his forehead to Tom's.

"Can I try?"

"Huh?"

"I want to see if I'd like it. I've been wondering… you know… what it would be like, taste like."

"You want to suck my cock?"

Tom nodded and kissed Alec again. "I'm still not hitting on you or anything. But we're mates and I'd rather ask you than go out and pull a stranger and end up in over my head getting my ass fucked."

"Okay." Alec looked at the clock. "I've got ten minutes now or we could leave it to next week and go on a date." Alec wiggled his eyebrows and Tom blushed again.

"Next week then. After work one evening?"

"Sure thing. We'll have more time and I can reciprocate if you're in the mood." Alec kissed his cheek and patted his ass. "Now, I have to get finished up here."

"Thanks, buddy. Have a great weekend."

Alec stopped to watch Tom leave. It would be a real pain if that started to get complicated. He was sure there was nothing more to Tom's question but innocent curiosity, but he'd need to be careful. He didn't want Tom deciding he was gay after all and announcing Alec as his true love.

"Ready to head home?"

Alec smiled as Hamilton stole an embrace and crushed up close behind. Alec shivered at Hamilton's warm breath on the nape of his neck.

"I'm jealous that you're making dates without me already. You don't even have your boy at home yet."

"Hardly a rival, Rick." He turned in the embrace to look into Hamilton's eyes. "The guy just wants to taste a cock. And it's your fault after that little stunt last week with the photos. I bet he's been stroking himself over them ever since."

"Mm, I know I would." Hamilton rubbed a hand between Alec's butt cheeks, and dropped it between his legs to grab his balls.

"We're in the open office. There'll be surveillance."

"And I happen to know that security this evening are regular Service clients. In fact, now that Tom has left we have the whole floor to ourselves." Hamilton's hand moved around and pulled at Alec's belt, unhooked his pants, and pulled the zipper down.

"You have got to me kidding me?"

"I'm sure they're watching. We should give them a show."

"Over my desk?"

Hamilton tugged down Alec's pants and shorts, and pushed

him forward over his desk, kicking his legs apart. *Fucking hell.* Alec couldn't breathe. He was so turned on, so completely consumed with the need that washed through him the room was going fuzzy. He heard Hamilton's pants drop, felt his hands prize Alec's cheeks apart, and winced pleasurably at the dribble of something which ran over his hole. Hamilton pushed in two fingers, once, twice, and then the head of his cock nudged against Alec's pucker.

"Seeing you kissing Tom was so hot, Alec. I have to have you now." Alec groaned as Hamilton pushed into him, breathing through the stretch. *Fucking amazing.* The pace was frantic, the thrusts so deep, Alec grunted with each one and his hands scrabbled over his desk for purchase. "Oh, hell," Hamilton gasped. "I'm coming already." And he let go, flooding Alec's body with his seed. Hamilton leaned over his back. "Damn, I don't think I've ever come so fast. I feel light headed."

Alec chuckled. "And I feel wet. Have you got a cloth handy? I'm not exactly equipped out here for impromptu fucks." He flinched as Hamilton dropped to his knees and ran a tongue over the trickle of cum that had splashed over Alec's thigh, following all the way up to lick over his hole.

"You can shower when we get home." Hamilton stood up and slapped Alec's ass. "Put it away, sweetness, or Jerry will be wanting a piece of you."

"Jerry?"

"Security supervisor. He uses the office boys a lot. A portion of security are members of the Order for obvious reasons. Actually, I'll introduce you to him on the way out. You can give him a blowjob. He'll like that after watching us fuck."

"You really think he was watching?"

"I made sure of it, darling. Would you like to watch the replay when we drop in?"

Fridays were officially becoming the days weird stuff happened. Alec watched himself being fucked by Hamilton over his own desk while taking the cock of the security guard who had recorded the session as far into his throat as he could manage. Jerry—six foot four of pure Irish muscle with piercing blue eyes and a multitude of tattoos—talked nonstop about the things he'd seen from his private lair. Suddenly he stalled and shot his load down Alec's throat. He patted Alec's head and offered him a tissue to wipe his chin.

"Very nice to meet you, young sir," Jerry said. "You stop by anytime now."

"Thank you, I will."

Alec was still a little stunned as Hamilton dragged him into the car and, unheeding of the chauffeur, proceeded to launch into a heavy petting session through the sticky Friday night traffic.

Sebastian had cooked up a storm in the kitchen. Several stir-fry dishes were on the menu, along with couscous, salad, and fresh-baked bread. He'd also made Brendon's favorite coffee and caramel ice cream, and a batch of chocolate sauce. If Brendon didn't know something was up that should have told him.

They finished their meal and Hamilton called order at the table. "Sebastian, fill everyone's glass. I have an announcement and a toast to make."

With the wine poured and everyone settled back in their chairs except Hamilton who stood and walked to Sebastian's side. He placed a hand on the boy's shoulder.

"Brendon, Dylan, as of this weekend Sebastian will move into Alec's apartment."

Brendon sat up straight. "I *knew* it. I knew something was going on."

"That's not all. It's time for you to say goodbye to Sebastian."

Brendon shot a glance at Sebastian, who looked down at his hands. "This is by way of being a celebratory meal and a farewell." Hamilton leaned down to unfasten Sebastian's wrist-bands. As he removed them Dylan made a small choking sound and reached for Sebastian's hand across the table. Hamilton reached down to kiss Sebastian's cheek. "I'll always love you," he said, and a tear rolled down Sebastian's cheek.

"Why?" said Dylan, squeezing Sebastian's hand tighter.

"Sebastian is to become Alec's houseboy."

"*No!*" Brendon slapped his hand over his mouth as if willing the words not to tumble out. "Sebastian you can't leave. I'm so sorry. I don't know why I'm mean to you, but please, don't go."

"It's okay, Brendon." Sebastian's voice was no more than a whisper. "I'm sure my new master will bring me to visit."

"I don't care, you belong with us. I've watched you grow up, you were so little when you came here."

"And now I'm not."

"So," Hamilton said, firmly. "Before we digress any further, I'd like you to raise your glasses and toast with me. To Alec and Sebastian, may you have a long and happy relationship as master and boy. Alec, I hand you my boy, that you may care for and comfort him, my wish is that he will serve you well, as he has me all these years. Sebastian I release you to your new master with my full blessing. Know that this will always be your home. To Alec and Sebastian."

Brendon and Dylan repeated the toast and sipped a little wine. As soon as he put his glass down, Dylan jumped out of his seat and hugged Sebastian with all his strength. "I'm going to miss you so much, baby. What am I going to do when Brendon's driving me nuts?"

"You'll still see me on weekends."

"But who will I fuck? I can't believe you're moving."

"Sebastian?" Brendon's bottom lip quivered. "Was it because of me? I do love you, I'm sorry I'm spoiled and such a brat. *Please* stay."

"It's just time, Brendon, and Alec will take good care of me."

Hamilton motioned for Alec to join him in another part of the room and they left the boys to their conversation. The hugs continued… tears followed.

"Did you have to remove his wrist-bands?"

"He isn't yours if he has them on, Alec. You have to shop for your own to put on him."

"Are you sure I'm ready for this?"

"It doesn't matter whether you are, Sebastian is. His willingness will bring out the natural master I've seen in you, Alec. Don't worry about anything. A day at a time. And remember, you can ask me anything."

"I thought Brendon would be happy."

"The boys have been together a long time. Sebastian is the baby. Once they realize he'll still be around every weekend they'll calm down."

"Master?" Brendon bowed his head to Hamilton.

"What is it?"

"I'd like to request your permission to ask Sebastian's new master if we can say goodbye to him properly?"

"Go ahead."

"Alec, I know it's your first night as Sebastian's master and you probably want him for yourself, but please, can he sleep in our bed? I want him close this one last time and I want to make love to him and…" he stopped to wipe away the tears before they fell.

"Brendon, of course you can. And he can come as often as he wants with you for tonight."

"You can join us."

"No, you boys have fun."

"Thanks, Alec." Brendon hugged him briefly. "I love you too, you know. I'm not worried that he's your boy, I just… I'm gonna to miss him."

146

"I know. But we'll be here every weekend, just as we are now."

"Can I call him whenever I want to?"

"Of course you can."

"Go on then, boys," Hamilton said. "For once, don't worry about clearing up the dinner things."

"Thank you, Master."

As they disappeared, Alec turned back to Hamilton with a grin. "I guess that means I'll be clearing up." He nudged Hamilton's arm.

"You can go and sit down, darling. I'll do it."

"Then I'll help."

It wasn't long before the unmistakable sounds of sex and pleasure were filtering through from the boys' room. Together, Hamilton and Alec made short work of clearing the table, loading the dishwasher, and tidying the kitchen. It was nice to curl up on the sofa together with the echoes of love resounding around the walls.

"You know," Hamilton said, crawling over Alec to sit on his lap. "I would say that fucking you over your desk today was one of the top five hottest moments of my long and varied sexual history."

"Mine too." Alec leaned in for a kiss. "What's your number one?"

"Do you really want to know?"

"Yes. Tell me what I have to live up to."

"The single, hottest night of sex I've ever had was making love to you for the first time. You're exquisite Alec, I don't know what it is about you, but I can't get enough and you burn right through to my soul."

"Every single hot and sexy moment I've had is with you, Rick. I don't ever want you to have had enough. I want you to keep coming back for more and more and more."

Kisses followed that slowly morphed into passion and fire. Their groans soon matched those from the other room, and all was well in their world.

Coming Home

By Sunday evening they managed to transfer all Sebastian's stuff to Alec's apartment. Alec ignored the exasperated comments about the state of the place and the lack of organization.

"How do you ever get ready for work? Where are your ironed shirts?"

"I iron as required."

"Where's the laundry hamper?"

Alec raised his arms out to the sides. "The floor is the best place to keep an eye on whether laundry needs doing. Welcome to my world Sebastian. I'm sorry it doesn't meet your impeccable standards." Alec stomped off to the living room and threw himself onto the sofa.

Sebastian was there a minute later crawling over his back with a line of sweet kisses. "I'm sorry, Master. Forgive me?"

"I can't do this, Sebastian. You should go back to the other apartment."

"Alec, no, please. I was out of line and I'm sorry. Don't throw me away because I made a mistake."

Alec rolled over and wrapped his arms around the trembling body. Sebastian reminded Alec of a whippet: when he was nervous his slight body shook with tension. "I'm not 'throwing you away.' I just want you to be happy."

"I *am* happy. It just takes time to adjust. You have no idea how completely…" Sebastian kissed Alec's chest, "…utterly…" moving down to his stomach, "…and overwhelmingly happy I am to be here." Sebastian pulled Alec's shorts down to reveal his growing erection and planted kisses up and down the shaft. "And to be yours."

"You like being mine?"

"Absolutely. Your wish is my command, Master."

"I like that idea."

"I can tell." Sebastian lavished some more tongue action on Alec's cock. "Can I put in my first request to be fucked by my Master?"

"You'll need to take off those stupid jeans."

Sebastian stood, and dropped his pants. He always went commando, when he wore clothes at all. "Done," he smiled. "Your next request, Master?" he said as he pulled off Alec's shorts so they were both naked.

"Let's just be us for today. Just like we wanted at Master's." Alec held out his hand and Sebastian slid over Alec's body. Alec could definitely get used to this. No orders, no permission, just following the tide of passion and the body's natural path to ecstasy.

Their cocks ground together in delicious friction. "Where's the lube?" Sebastian was squirming already and Alec could feel his own climax closing in on him.

"Fuck, I have lube here." Alec grabbed a sachet off the end table. "Condoms are in the bathroom."

"Just lube, then." Sebastian grinned. He took the sachet from Alec, tore it open, and coated Alec's cock.

"Sebastian, we ought to play safe." The thought sobered him and, though he was still hard, the imminent climax abated.

"Alec, honey, I'm clean as a whistle and I'm betting you are too seeing you always bareback with Master. I'd really like our time together to be special, nothing between us. We can use them when we fuck around other people but I want all of you." He waited, lube packet still in hand, the pretty green eyes Alec loved so much wide and innocent.

"I've never fucked anyone without one."

"Neither have I."

"You've never been fucked without one?"

"When I was young and stupid. But I promise you I'm clean. I wouldn't put you at risk."

At a flutter of Sebastian's eyelashes, Alec caved in. "Okay," he said with a return of enthusiasm. They took a little time working back up to that moment where the desire for penetration became desperate. Alec rolled them over carefully so they didn't end up on the floor and rested over Sebastian.

"Take me, Master." Sebastian wrapped his legs around Alec's hips and Alec guided his cock to Sebastian's sweet little pucker. He nudged against it, watched him stretch to accommodate the head before swallowing it inside his body. Fuck, it felt good. "More." Sebastian wriggled beneath him and Alec leaned over to find his lips and in the process his whole cock disappeared inside Sebastian. They groaned in unison. "That feels amazing. You are amazing." Alec mashed his mouth against Sebastian's and took up a steady motion of his hips, slow withdraw, fast thrust. He was close already but he wanted to make it last and last. He pulled out and sat up on the sofa. He tugged Sebastian to sit astride his lap, facing him. So much extra sensation as he slipped back up into that ass. They rocked together and Alec smoothed firm hands over Sebastian's chest and tweaked his nipples, smiling at the yelp and increased speed of his gyrating.

"I'm close, Master," he said, increasing the friction on his cock against Alec's belly.

"Come when you're ready, Sebastian, it's just me and you."

"Alec, fuck, fuck, *fuck*." And he spilled over Alec's body. His ass muscles clenched around the cock inside him to pull Alec over the edge with the last few frantic thrusts as they crushed themselves together. They stayed, wrapped in each other's arms, as their breathing settled, and the last of the shudders subsided.

"I've never done that before." Alec squeezed Sebastian closer.

"Come at the same time?"

"No, have sex for me rather than Master." He kissed Sebastian's neck and shoulders, nipping at the skin. "It's like you're my first all over again."

"You are just the sweetest thing." Sebastian nuzzled into the hollow of Alec's neck. "Sweet and funny and gorgeous... and sticky."

"It is sticky, but the shower... well, it's too small for both of us."

"Don't be stupid, I'm tiny, besides I can kneel at your feet if necessary. We shower together." Sebastian pulled Alec to his feet and pushed him through to the bathroom. Somewhere the roles of master and boy had already started to tangle together.

The shower turned out to be plenty big enough to wash and fuck. Alec was feeling particularly sated as he stretched out on the sofa afterward, naked and almost dry. "Do you mind if I shop tomorrow while you're at work?" Sebastian flopped onto the sofa next to Alec. "I've got the week off to move," Sebastian added. "I could pick up a few things."

And an interesting week it would be too. Alec could see himself coming home each day to an apartment gradually transformed from chaos to order, having to ask where things were and generally just getting in the way in his own home.

"Anything in particular?"

"Food for one thing. It would be helpful if I know what evenings you'll be here and when I should please myself."

"I guess we should talk about boundaries too. This is going to be as new for you as it is for me and I know you've never lived full time in the role you had with Master. We need to find a balance that works. You could start by telling me what you think you need from me."

Sebastian gave the matter serious consideration. After a minute, nodding to himself, he said, "Respect is the first. Don't take me for granted. Ask me anything and tell me if you're not sure about how to handle something I've done or if I've made a mistake. The biggest thing for me is knowing where I stand. I need to know if there's anything that's off limits."

"Such as?"

"I'm a neat-freak, Alec. But if you don't want me to keep the place clean and tidy and organize stuff you have to tell me. All I ask is that you give me one space that I can call mine to escape to."

"I want you to be happy. If that means you want to go through this place on your hands and knees with a toothbrush, do it. Just don't throw anything away without checking and make sure you know where something's going to be when I need it."

"Are you sure?"

"I cope with clean and tidy at Master's. Who knows, I might even learn a bit of upkeep myself. As for your own space, well, this is your home now—it's all your space. But if you specifically want to take over the office room that's fine and we'll have a rule that if you're in there with the door closed you're having private time."

"Same with you then and the bedroom?"

"I guess. It's good to be able to get out of each other's way in the early days."

"I prefer to cook every day. If you give me a list of your favorite dishes I can include them in my meal plan."

Alec laughed quietly. "You have a meal plan?"

"Don't tell me you're one of those annoying people that can eat anything but stays in shape. Damn it. I'm a natural tubby. It takes a lot of restraint and yoga for me to stay this size."

"I go to the gym regularly but you know something? A few extra pounds wouldn't hurt."

Sebastian looked horrified. "You don't like my body?"

"Oh, baby, of course I do. I'm just saying you're on the slender side of toned." They hadn't even gone through the basic boundaries chat and Alec had already put his foot in it. He could see the shock on Sebastian's face, that maybe he wasn't what Alec wanted. "Sebastian, I love your body. What I'm saying, badly, is that you don't have to work so hard to keep me happy. I would love fucking you anyway."

"Easy to say when I don't have an ounce of body fat. Wait till my ass is jiggling in your hands when you're pounding me or my hips disappear into love handles."

"Is that really going to happen overnight?"

"I like having a meal plan. I like structure and order in my life."

"Meal plan it is then. Whatever you need to be happy."

There was a definite slumping of shoulders. "You're going to get fed up with me in five minutes. I'm such a dweeb."

"I won't. If you can live with me dropping my clothes all over the floor I'm sure I can manage with a meal plan. As long as there's beer in the fridge and chocolate in the cupboard, I'm happy."

"I can make chocolate." Sebastian draped himself cock-down over Alec's lap. If they were going to be naked all evening during the week, like they were at Hamilton's all weekend, it would be hard to resist Sebastian's charms. Alec tried to concentrate on the conversation, smoothing his hand over the globe of Sebastian's ass. He was right, not an ounce of fat, it was all firm muscle under Alec's hand. "Once I find my way around the kitchen I'll get the ingredients in. What's your favorite?"

"Green and Blacks Butterscotch."

"Mine will be better." Sebastian rolled over seductively.

"I have died and gone to heaven and you are my angel. The way to my heart is definitely through my stomach."

"Say, no more. I'm on it." And he was indeed—on Alec's cock, with his bare ass kneading it to life again already. He stretched up for a kiss and Alec surrendered himself to the passion that spilled over. It looked like they'd be having a lot of sex and a lot of showers. Alec certainly wasn't complaining. It was more of a leisurely, teasing fuck than the passion from earlier or the frantic thrashing in the shower.

"I should buy you wrist-bands once we've settled." The slow, sensual movements were eating away at Alec's brain.

"I'd like that, Master. I feel naked without them and I want people to know I'm yours."

"Soon, then. We'll go see that Maurice guy."

"Thank you, Master."

"I've never come so much, Sebastian. I love not having to fight it with you."

"Will we always be so free?"

"I have other commitments, and on weekends we'll be at Master's."

"Just sometimes?"

"We can have special days for us, with no scene, no master or boy. Would you like that?"

"Yes, Master."

Alec held Sebastian's hips steady and looked at him. "Sebastian, do you fuck other people, like at work or anything?"

Sebastian wrapped his arms around Alec's neck and nuzzled into him. "Sometimes. During the week we used to please ourselves."

"Do you have a boyfriend?"

It was a delightful chuckle that burbled against Alec's neck. "I belong to you. There's no one else, Master. Guys hit on me when I'm out sometimes and if I'm in the mood I'll go with it. There's nothing regular. Master was my life and now you are. I don't need anyone else."

"You're sure? I don't think I like the idea of you fucking other people. Your ass is mine. I'll be your Master and offer you for service but if I'm not with you, you're a sex-free zone."

154

"Yes, Master. I understand. Do you want to finish fucking or shall we chat some more?"

"I think my wiener needs a little time to recover."

Sebastian peeled himself off Alec's wilting cock and sprawled out over his lap. "You're so sexy, Master. I love being here already."

"I hope you won't be lonely. Work's really busy at the moment. I see Master two evenings a week and this week I'm going out for the evening with a friend from work." Tom. That seemed like a million miles away right now.

"I'll be okay. You have a massive TV, internet, and a ton of DVDs and books, and I have loads to do around the house this week. Your ironing is taking over the office and I have to find space for my clothes."

"Do you have any? You're always naked. I figured you had one pair of jeans and that's it."

"I wear a suit to work, Master."

Sebastian in a suit. The thought jerked his dick awake again. It put a mouth-watering picture in Alec's mind. Sebastian leaning over the desk in the office, suit jacket pulled up, pants around his ankles, and that tight little ass in Alec's hands as he rammed him from behind. "I think I'd like to see that."

"You will next week."

"What do you do?"

"I work for a mapping company, digitizing aerial photographs and processing satellite data."

"You what?"

"I turn aerial photos and satellite images into maps and digital elevation models for industry. Think Google Earth. I'd really like to update your desktop pc if that's okay. It means I'll be able to work from home occasionally."

"Sure, tell me what you need and I'll get it."

"I can buy my own computer, Master. They do pay me. Actually, we should talk about bills and stuff too. I'm happy to pay my way."

"Oh no you don't." Alec sat up straighter. "You're my boy, Sebastian. You work part time so that you're here for me when I want you."

"Just saying. I'm good at accounts and stuff if you want me to take care of the household finances. You must have enough of that at work."

"Now that would be useful. I hate dealing with bills. My investments portfolio is sound but day-to-day things drive me crazy."

"Consider it done."

"Okay. I'm going to have to get some sleep. Early start tomorrow. Come on, let's go to bed."

"Thank you, Master."

Alec finished their fuck in the middle of the night when he woke up with Sebastian's leg draped over his hip and realized he didn't have to wait for someone to tell him he could. Sebastian was his. He could initiate sex as often as he wanted. The simplest of things to most people and yet beyond Alec's reach until now. He definitely intended to make the most of it.

Tom

"Run ragged" described Alec's current condition. The week was well and truly launched and Alec had spent too much of it on his knees and not enough at his desk. How he was supposed to keep on top of such high-profile accounts when there was an endless merry-go-round of cocks to service, he just didn't know.

Four of his new clients came back for blowjobs and to watch him fuck Michael. Worthington was also becoming a regular. Plus, he had to keep Hamilton topped up with morning and lunchtime fucks. Alec felt exhausted. Monday he'd calmed a fretful Sebastian because the boy worried he'd over tidied. Tuesday saw him sacrificed again to Hamilton's insatiable appetite—the man could fuck for hours—and now today, Wednesday, he was heading out with Tom for their little tête à tête. Alec was beginning to wonder if his dick would fall off from over use. But, he'd promised Tom it would be this week and his friend was already skittish as hell around him. It was definitely a case of getting it over with.

Six o'clock. He'd been in the office since seven. Tom waited as Alec locked away his files and shut down his computer. Alec couldn't resist running his hand over Tom's ass as they walked out of the office. It surprised him a bit that Tom didn't flinch. Maybe he thought it was an accident. In the elevator, Alec made a more obvious grab for it. He was stunned as Tom leaned back against him rather than shaking him off.

"Where are you taking me?" Alec said, as they left the building.

"I thought we'd grab a bite to eat and then head over to my place. Is that okay?"

"Sounds great." And it actually did. Alec was already starting to relax in Tom's company. There was no pressure and no expectations with him, other than having to hand over his cock for ten minutes, but it wasn't in the same way as work, or Hamilton, or even Sebastian.

They enjoyed a light bar meal and a few too many beers. Laughed about work, Chloe's tangled love life, and Alec's crush on the boss. Then Tom got serious. "Alec, I don't want to put any limitations on tonight."

"What does that mean?"

"I don't know. Just… see where it goes, okay?"

"You don't have free entry to my back door, sweetheart, if that's what you're hinting at."

Tom seemed thoughtful.

Fuck, he's really been thinking we'd have full sex.

He was a nice enough guy, just not one Alec would go for under any circumstances other than the one they were in—a mate helping out a mate. And besides, Alec still felt bad about the whole blowjob thing, as though he'd forced Tom's hand and now the guy was in a place he wouldn't have been otherwise: questioning his sexuality. It was obvious from Tom's history the potential was there, but without Alec's interference, he would have gone on with his girlfriend and been happy enough.

"Are you ready?" Tom asked. He looked bashful.

"Sure." Alec slugged the last of his beer and welcomed the warm buzz in his body. He did feel good. He let himself lean into Tom as they walked from the bar and Tom surprised him again by reaching for his hand. They ambled the few blocks to Tom's apartment and at some point that Alec didn't quite remember, Tom's arm had slipped around Alec's waist. He only noticed when Tom removed it to unlock the door.

They both shucked out of suit jackets and then Tom was on him, lips crashing into his, tongue forcing entry, and Alec just let go and gave his body permission to do what it wanted. Tom pinned him to the wall and pulled at his shirt and tie. "You're so damn sexy, Alec."

"Whoa, sweetheart. Since when has this been about you being hungry for me?" Alec spun around as Tom stripped him out of his shirt and used the tie, still around his neck, to pull him into another scorching kiss. *Useful tool. I'll have to remember it when I fuck Sebastian next week with his suit on.*

Tom stripped off his own shirt, toed off his shoes, and reached for Alec's belt. "I just want to taste you," he mumbled. He fell to his knees, forcing Alec back against the wall again. Alec's mind skipped a step and the next thing he knew his cock was disappearing into Tom's mouth.

"Fuck, that's good. Damn, Tom, are you sure you haven't done that before?" Alec thought Tom was grinning, the best he could tell anyway while the guy had a cock in his mouth. He sucked on the end as his hands pulled off Alec's shoes, socks and the rest of his clothes. Alec hadn't had any intentions of getting naked, of being here long. How had this happened? And Tom was good, driving him forward into dangerous realms of wanting more than he should. Alec's body was programmed differently these days. Hot blowjobs were a precursor to sex, either fucking or being fucked. One was out of the question and somehow, Alec felt fucking Tom probably wasn't the best idea. But that's where it was heading, in Alec's mind at least. It was time to stop it or push on. He needed to make a decision fast but his mind was fuzzy from too much beer.

Tom let up for a moment and gave Alec a chance to catch his breath. He pulled Alec through the apartment to the bedroom. "Tom, we need to slow down, mate. What's going on?" But he wasn't listening. He peeled off the rest of his clothes and pushed Alec onto the bed, suctioning his lips over Alec's balls and grasping his cock with firm strokes. "You are a fucking liar, Tom Parsons," Alec chuckled. "Tell me where you're going with this or I'll just flip you over and fuck you into the mattress."

Tom let go of Alec's cock and crawled over his body, running his tongue over it as he made his way up. He nipped at Alec's lips and throat and Alec groaned, surrendering into his hands. "That's exactly where I was going with it," he whispered in Alec's ear. "Condoms and lube are to your right."

Alec pushed himself onto his elbows and grabbed Tom on his slither back down Alec's body. "You really want me to fuck you?"

"Don't you want to?"

"It wasn't my plan for the evening. Tom, I don't want things to get weird between us at work."

His hands were still working over Alec's cock, wearing away his resistance and the logical part of his brain that said this was not the best plan of action. "Chloe manages okay and she's fucked half the office. It's just mates, helping each other out."

"There is no shortage of sex in my life and as far as I was aware you have a girlfriend."

"Good for you, Alec. But I'm a little short in the man-love department and at the moment, I'm aching for it. I don't want to pull a stranger. I trust you."

"Wait, Tom, knock that off a minute. We have to talk about this." Tom let go of Alec's cock and sat cross-legged on the bed. "You want me to be your first?" Too many weird thoughts were running through Alec's head about Hamilton and what first times should be and Alec was *not* going there with Tom.

"Technically, no. I fucked a couple of guys in uni and yeah, they fucked me but that was five years ago, Alec. I just want you to grease the wheels for me, see if it's something I want to get back into or a passing phase."

Grease the wheels indeed. What Tom didn't take into account was the monumental leap this would be for Alec—his first fuck outside of "office boys" and houseboys. Another level of virginity. Alec flopped back against the bed. It would be so easy to do, but would it be fair? "Tom, you should know I have a boyfriend." Not exactly true, but as good as any explanation could be, given the reality.

"Regular? Since when?"

"He lives with me."

"Fucking hell, Alec, I wouldn't have asked you if I'd realized. What in the hell are you doing here then, and the beejay the other week, what was *that* about?"

"He knows where I am. We fuck other people. I just wanted you to know the situation before we do this. I'm not necessarily going to be around for you whenever you need a fix."

"So he won't mind if we..."

"No he won't. We don't have secrets. He knows I came out with you for a purpose. If we do have sex I'll tell him when I get home."

Tom leaned back over Alec and pressed his lips in a tender kiss. "Is he cute?"

"Sweetheart, he's hot as hell."

"Can I meet him?"

"No."

The grinding of hips and trailing fingernails were reawakening the fire in Alec's belly. "Is that why you said I couldn't fuck you?"

"Yeah. It's our thing. I fuck others, he gets fucked by others but only he fucks me." Another white lie which should tide him over. What Alec didn't know was how he'd tell Hamilton he'd fucked Tom.

"So, theoretically I could bump into him in the street and end up fucking him?"

"I guess. Enough about Sebastian, Tom. What are *we* going to do right now? Because if you keep that up, you're going to have to finish me, one way or another."

"I think, you talk too much." And that was that. Alec let Tom take the reins right up until the moment he slid into Tom's ass with a groan and did exactly what he said he'd do—Alec fucked him deep and hard into the mattress. And from where Alec was, it looked like Tom loved every fucking minute of it.

Inner Strength

Tom was a man of his word. Other than the odd innuendo and brush of his hand when they were alone, everything was in good order at work. Alec appreciated the quiet support and even passed him a few of his older accounts so that he could concentrate on the big cheeses. Tom also exhibited an underlying no-nonsense persona more and more, which Alec had never noticed before but now appreciated. It was a nice aside from the rest of his mad life.

And in another transformation, Sebastian morphed from timid slave boy into powerhouse businessman when he donned a suit. It was a potent aphrodisiac and Alec was glad Sebastian only worked a couple of days a week otherwise he'd be on very shaky legs. Life was definitely settling down. Alec hadn't seen a new cock in over a week, or was it two? And his regulars fell into a neat pattern that allowed him enough time to put in some real office hours. Weekends were still the best. Brendon and Dylan continued affectionate and pampering of Sebastian, and Hamilton always seemed to have a little something special for Alec.

At home, Sebastian had indeed transformed the apartment into a thing of order and beauty. Alec had no idea the place possessed so much potential and he was convinced Sebastian had single-handedly added a good few grand to its value just by implementing a little Feng Shui.

What preyed most on Alec's mind was the need to follow through with the handover of Sebastian from Hamilton and place his owner-ship bands on Sebastian. Sebastian was being very patient and wasn't pushing too much, but the suggestion that they might have time to shop together grew more frequent. Alec knew he was being stupid, stalling when everything else was working so well, but it was as if claiming Sebastian officially for the world to see was a step too far at the moment. He just couldn't picture himself going into the shop and interacting with Maurice as a master instead of a boy.

The turning point came as Miles Henry arrived unannounced to invite Alec to lunch. He obviously had the inside loop on Hamilton's diary because the boss was out of the office. Alec cringed when he saw Henry head toward his desk but he was determined to stand his ground. He took a deep breath and shifted into the frame of mind he used with Sebastian and, if he thought about it, his account clients before the Order had infiltrated his work.

"Alec, I understand the Master's away. What say you to a little lunch play?"

Ha-fucking-ha, jerk-off. Alec stood to give his hand as brief a shake as possible. "Mr. Henry, it's nice of you to drop by but I'm afraid I'm not available at the moment."

"Oh? How so? You are standing right here and you have to eat." Henry glanced around the rest of the office. "Why don't we take this discussion to Hamilton's office? I have some figures I want to run by you for the project anyway."

It wasn't unusual for Alec to use Hamilton's office to service his clients but he didn't really want to be alone with Miles Henry without someone to guard his back—literally. But he couldn't see a way out of it. "I'll be right with you, sir, if you'd like to go ahead."

Still with Henry in earshot, Alec turned to Tom. "Tom, can you contact my next appointment and tell them I'll be a few minutes late?"

Tom smiled his conspirator's smile. "Certainly, Mr. Caldwell. Can I bring you some coffee?"

Henry glanced briefly over his shoulder but continued on to the office. "Thanks buddy." Alec smiled back. "That asshole thinks he can walk in here whenever he wants and I'll drop everything for him."

"Even your pants?" Tom winked but it just wasn't funny. "Tell him straight, Alec. You're not a lapdog. Outline your duties and he can take 'em or leave 'em."

"Will do."

It was a long walk to the office and Alec didn't want to close and lock the door, but he did. If the guy wanted a blowjob, he could have one but there would be no lunch and no fucking. It helped that Alec had more understanding of how the Order worked. He knew the rules backed him up even if there wasn't another person present to do so.

"Mr. Henry," Alec said with a smile. "Can I offer you coffee?"

"Call me Miles, Alec, and you know damn well why I'm here. I've been waiting for your call."

"You're not one of my regular Service clients, sir. I have no reason to contact you."

"Stop playing games with me." It was definitely a powerplay he was going for. "If it means taking you in the office, I will. Take off your clothes."

Alec sighed. The prattish attitude made the next part easier. "Mr. Henry, as a Level One Service Trainee you can only request oral sex from me and it should be incorporated with some kind of business association. I have serviced you in the past at the willingness of my master. He's not here to verify that it's still his wish for me to do so, though on this occasion I am willing to forgo that and offer you oral sex, in good faith for your friendship with my master." Alec paused to let his words sink in. "You have no right to demand anything else of me and I am unwilling to give it of my own free will. I hope we understand each other and that this will not become an awkward situation." *There, fucker, what do you make of that?*

"Well, well, it seems the slave boy has found a backbone." Henry moved in, pressed Alec against the wall, and groped his crotch. "But I must insist you present your ass, young man. *Nobody* teases me and gets away with it. I *am* going to fuck you and you *are* going to enjoy it."

"No." Alec ignored the fact Henry had already unzipped his pants and was delving around inside. "Any attempt you make will be against my will and I have no qualms about informing the authorities."

Henry stepped back and considered Alec. He looked as though he was weighing up the likelihood of Alec actually calling his bluff. Whatever he found in his appraisal changed his attitude. "I thank you, Mr. Caldwell, for making your position clear. I will leave you to your business and trust you'll have a good afternoon." He offered his hand, which Alec shook, and then left.

Alec locked the door and leaned against it. He was shaking. He slid to the floor and wrapped his arms around his knees. *Fucking hell. What a bastard.* A few minutes later, there came a knock on the door. Alec stood and straightened his clothes, putting everything back where it should be, and opened it.

"Is everything okay, Alec?" Tom looked around the office. Alec grabbed his arm and pulled him in. He locked the door behind him.

"You were right." Alec leaned against Tom and lowered his head to his shoulder. "The bastard came on to me, started touching me up and expected me to drop my pants."

Tom enfolded Alec in a hug. Strong arms supported his shaking body. "Fucking hell. No wonder you're trembling. You didn't though, did you?"

Alec snorted. "Give me some credit. He wasn't here five minutes. I sent him packing."

"Who is he anyway?"

"A business associate of Hamilton's."

"He doesn't work here? Damn, you could have reported him. I've heard things like this happen but I always thought it was women that got the raw end of the deal. Sit down. I'll get you a coffee. Do you think Hamilton will mind if I use his fancy machine?"

"He won't mind." Alec sat on the sofa, grabbed a cushion and hugged it to his chest. "It's never happened to me before. I thought he was going to force me."

Tom put two cups of coffee on the table. He sat next to Alec and held him close. How would Tom have reacted if they hadn't had sex? Alec betted exactly the same as he had just done. Tom Parsons was without doubt one of life's genuine good guys.

"You know, Tom, if you didn't have Emma and I didn't have Sebastian, I think we'd be ideally suited."

Tom chuffed amusement deep in his chest. "It's you falling for my charm now is it? You are lovely," he said in a more serious tone. "I'd date you in a heartbeat but … I don't think we're suited really."

"No?"

"You're a great guy but you fuck around. I know, technically I did too, but it was a one-off and Emma knew I was going to try it. Now it's back to just me and her. I don't play the field and I wouldn't want my partner to either."

Alec thought about that. What would it be like to have just one lover, and for them to be just his? But he had no concept of it. The first time he fucked someone it was a threesome in this very office and Hamilton was probably fucking some "office boy" right now. Sebastian's ass was open season even though he was now only fucking with Alec's permission. "I've never been asked to do it so I don't know if it's something I'd want."

"You've never had a monogamous relationship?"

Before Alec could answer, his phone buzzed. "Oh shit, Hamilton's back. He wants to know why he can't get into his office."

Tom groaned. "That man is going to think there's something going on between us."

"There is." Alec kissed Tom on the cheek. "Stay there, he'll be cool. I'll have to tell him about Henry."

"You're not."

Alec opened the door.

"Ah, I don't have to call the locksmith then." Hamilton paused when he saw Tom and the coffee cups. His regard looked dangerous. "Am I interrupting something?"

"I do apologize Mr. Hamilton," Alec said with grave formality. "I had a bit of a scare and Tom was supporting me."

Hamilton gazed at Tom but addressed Alec with concern in his voice. "Is everything all right?"

Tom stood. "Can I leave you to it?" he said. Alec nodded and Tom patted his shoulder before he left.

"What happened?"

"Miles Henry turned up for my ass. When I said no, he threatened to take it. Don't panic," Alec said at the anger which swept across Hamilton's face. "I showed him the door politely, but I confess, I was a bit shaken once he'd left. Tom's a good friend. He was only sitting with me while I caught my breath."

"I thought I saw the rotten bastard in the lobby,. I'll need to speak to Harrison."

"Bossman Harrison? Why?"

"Because Harrison is a leading member of the Order and Henry has done it before."

"Raped office boys?"

"Not raped, but think about it. If you and I weren't so close, if you weren't my houseboy as well as my office boy, would you have had the courage to stand up to him?"

Alec thought for a second, and shook his head.

"You'd have let him have his way, thought you had no recourse. It sets a bad example and is not what the Order is about. We do not exist to feed a power rush. His attitude needs to be addressed."

"You're right. If I didn't have the confidence in you to stand by me I wouldn't have stood my ground."

"Did he touch you?"

Alec shrugged a negative, as much to convince himself as Hamilton. "Only a quick grope. I actually offered him a blowjob but he didn't take me up on it."

"You are to have no further sexual contact with him. I'm so sorry I wasn't here for you, but perhaps it came at a good time."

"It did. If I can stand up to him as a member of the Order, then I'm ready to be a master. It's time I saw Maurice about Sebastian's bands."

Hamilton kissed Alec tenderly. "I'm so proud of you. We should do something special this weekend… and you owe Tom another blowjob."

"Is that a direct request or it is optional? Because he's told me that however much he appreciates my services, he's committed from here on in to be faithful to his girlfriend."

"In that case, a non-sexual treat is in order. Does he like sports?"

"I believe he's an Arsenal fan and oh, he's cricket mad."

"Cricket it is then. I'll arrange for some tickets for the Captain's Lounge at Lords. There's bound to be an international coming up."

"Are you a cricket fan?"

"In my youth."

"There's so much I don't know about you."

"And much I don't know about you, darling. But we'll get there. What's the rush? I'll let you know later today and you can let Tom know."

"Thanks, Rick."

"For what?"

"For looking after those who look after me."

Hamilton kissed Alec's hand. "Making sure you're cared for is my priority, Alec. Now do you want to take the rest of the day off?"

"I'm fine, really. I'd rather stay close to you."

"Then let's have lunch. I'll take you out."

What Alec appreciated more than the offer of lunch out or tickets for Tom was the fact that Hamilton, though likely back early for a lunchtime fuck, had done no more than hold Alec's face in his hand. It was a boost for Alec's confidence. Hamilton really did care for him and did see him as more than a piece of ass and that, to Alec, was worth the world.

When he heard about his treat later that afternoon, Tom threw his arms around Alec's neck and kissed him in front of the whole office. It got them a cheer and a standing ovation, to which they both bowed. Several of their colleagues asked when the wedding would be and if they could attend. Others wanted to know exactly what they had to do to get into Alec's good graces to earn the right to free hospitality tickets to sports events, and there were a few too many innuendos for Alec's comfort.

Despite the excitement, all Alec wanted and looked forward to was getting home to Sebastian.

A New Master and a New Boy

Excitement spurred Alec's feet along the hallway to his front door. Sebastian rushed to greet him like a happy puppy. The boy jumped into his arms and slid down his body to kiss the bump of his cock and then his feet. "Master!" He beamed happily and sat back on his heels.

"As much as I love you naked, sweetness, you'll need to get dressed. We're going shopping." Alec wiggled his brows. Sebastian tilted his head and stared up for a moment.

"Your dinner is almost ready, Master. Would you like me to serve first or shall I turn off the oven?"

"Should you be using the oven or the stove without clothes? I don't want any accidents. I'm very fond of your cock."

"I'm very careful. And I use an apron."

"Let's eat first."

Alec's apartment was nice but it had nothing on Hamilton's. The whole flat would fit in Hamilton's private living room with space left over. The dining nook off the kitchen was more than ample for two, though, and Sebastian always laid the table formally, with glasses, side plates, cutlery for several courses, candles, and a flower. Every time Alec saw it he had to stop and kiss him, it made him feel special, cared for and in an odd way loved by his little houseboy. Alec had strong feelings for Sebastian but he wasn't sure what they were. He certainly wouldn't want to be without him and not just because of the cooking, cleaning, and endless supply of freshly laundered shirts. Alec loved his company, his humor, and most of all his affection. The sex was great, and Alec was getting used to the way Sebastian liked to touch, caress, and cuddle.

"So where are we going?" Dinner over, Sebastian's eagerness was infectious. He checked his hair in the hall mirror. "Am I dressed appropriately?"

Alec leaned his chin on Sebastian's shoulder and peered at his lover's reflection. Contemporary-cut skinny jeans in the darkest blue, a close-fitting, pale-orange Oxford shirt and a navy preppy cardigan. A fringed scarf and distressed Derby boots completed the look. "You always look fab. Besides I don't intend for you to keep those clothes on long."

Sebastian spun around, his excitement bubbling over and he bounced up and down. "Seriously? You're taking me on our first master-boy session? Master, thank you, thank you. I'm so looking forward to being able to serve you properly."

Well, fuck. That hadn't been quite the response he was going for. It looked like Alec had been failing in his role as master in several ways. Maurice was a definite, and maybe there would be a few customers, given the time of day, so Alec could get Sebastian a few fucks while they were there. "Well, don't get too excited. We're going to see about your bracelets. You'll be naked to try them on. We'll have to wait and see what happens after that."

Sebastian dragged him out the door. It wasn't far on the tube but Sebastian got a lot of attention. Alec had actually never really been out with him. It was a strange feeling. Sort of proud and yet not quite. A rowdy group of completely camp lads were all over each other and spending too much time checking out Sebastian's ass. Alec grabbed it and pulled him in close to whoops and cheers and Sebastian cuddled against Alec's chest. "Thank you, Master," he whispered. "I feel safe with you."

"I'll always look after you, baby."

Maurice's store was quiet. Alec had phoned ahead to make sure they would be alone to chat. He didn't think he could face anyone else being able to overhear his first fumbling attempts at being a master.

"Ah, here you are," Maurice said in greeting as they stepped through the door. "And the beautiful Sebastian. How are you both this evening?"

"Very well, thank you. Did you find anything suitable?"

Maurice preened. "I think I've found just the thing."

"Remove your clothes please?" Alec ordered Sebastian. "You can put them in the changing room."

"Master." Sebastian bowed his head and walked through the arch to the back of the shop.

"I should tell you we can get busy of an evening. You know I'm happy for my customers to be open. I only tell you so that you can be prepared."

"Thanks, Maurice. I'm still very new to this role. Sebastian is being very patient with me but I think he's feeling the need to stretch his legs a little."

"He used to be Hamilton's boy, didn't he?"

"Yes, and used regularly for entertainment. I'm yet to find a suitable avenue for that to happen."

"I'm sure if you're here a while, an opportunity will present itself. I have several rooms available should you need one, all equipped with the necessaries. Now, what do you think of these?"

Maurice opened a long box and presented it to Alec. The bed of pale blue silk held three matching chains, two for the wrists and a longer, thicker collar. Alec picked up the necklace and ran it through his hands. Two elongated links connected to two smaller almost circular ones repeated all the way around and in the palest gold, he'd ever seen. Not quite white and not quite yellow. "They're beautiful."

Sebastian returned, sporting a nicely swelling cock, and took up his place at Alec's feet, "Master," he said, bending to kiss Alec's shoe.

"They're extra small, so they should be a perfect fit."

"What do think, Sebastian?"

As the boy looked up and caught sight of the bands, his breath caught and his eyes filled. "Master, are those really for me?"

"Do you like them?"

"They're gold. They're amazing."

"You're very special, Sebastian. I want you to remember that whenever you look at them."

Alec fixed the collar around Sebastian's neck and Sebastian raised his hands so that Alec could fit the bracelets. They were perfectly snug and the color was just right against Sebastian's creamy skin. He was one of the only boys Alec had seen that didn't go for tanning. The look suited him, gave him an ethereal glow. With his slight frame, fine blond hair, and pale green eyes, he was almost elfin. Right now, all Alec could see were the lightly parted full lips which begged to be kissed. He pulled him to stand and pressed his mouth against them. *Beautiful.*

At that moment, the door opened and a group of gentlemen entered. Maurice greeted each by name. One entered into a discussion with Maurice about their needs while two headed toward the rubberwear section at the rear of the store. The last, a tall, well-built guy, easily in his late thirties, took up a seat and seemed to be appraising Sebastian. Maurice excused himself for a moment to Alec and led the gentleman he'd been speaking to toward a display rack and began discussing its contents.

"That's a beautiful boy you have," the seated man said to Alec.

"Thank you, I'm very fond of him."

"Of legal age?"

Alec nodded and the man continued his appraisal of Sebastian. Alec wasn't sure whether he should say anything else or go about his own business. The man smiled and turned his attention to his companion, deep in conversation with Maurice. "Tristan, come and see this boy. He has a good cock on him."

Alec covered Sebastian's body as he began to tremble. "Are you okay?"

"Yes, Master." He reached up to whisper in Alec's ear. "I like it when you show me off, it makes me feel sexy and that I'm a good boy for you."

Alec kissed his cheek. "I understand."

Tristan came to stand with them. "Is the boy shy?"

"No. I was checking if he was cold."

Tristan offered his hand. "I'm Tristan, this is Freddie," gesturing to the man sitting down, "The two out back are Giorgio and Phillip. Maurice has been a godsend to us for a number of years."

"Alexander, and this is Sebastian." Sebastian bowed.

"We're going to a party. It's a very small, select gathering. Do you think you would be interested in attending with your boy? You don't have to say now. Once we leave you can ask Maurice for an honest reference and decide in your own time." Tristan handed Alec a business card. "That's the address and my number. Call me if you want to join us. No more than eight plus yourselves. Free entry."

"Will there be other boys?"

"Yes, two others. Rio is the most delicious redhead you've ever seen and Milo is purebred Italian, dark and brooding. Sebastian would be the perfect accompaniment and a rare delight indeed. He's the finest I've seen in a long time."

It was one of those bizarre conversations that Alec was getting used to and for some reason he liked Tristan. The guy was about the same age as Freddie, but smaller built, the same height as Alec, and he had a genuine air about him. "Thank you. Would you like to play with him?"

"Ah, what a delight that would be. But, do define play for me, before I overstep my invitation." Tristan's smile was bright and friendly. Yes, Alec felt comfortable with him, the same as he had with Dicky and Worthington.

"Let me turn that around for you. What would you like to do?"

"Touch a little to begin with, see how he feels, then probe a little. It would be a nice starter before the party."

"Then you may play." Alec smiled.

Tristan raised an eyebrow and took a step closer to Sebastian. "Come out from behind your Master, sweetie. I won't hurt you."

Sebastian stepped to the side and lowered his head with a blush. He was sporting a very impressive erection with nowhere to hide it. His hands were behind his back, his feet slightly apart.

"Oh my, Freddie, will you look at that. A fine example, indeed." Tristan slipped to his knees and wrapped his mouth around the head of Sebastian's cock. Sebastian took in a deep breath. Alec didn't think either of them had expected the guy to suck him off. Sebastian kept his pose. His lips parted and his breath hitched every now and then. "Delicious," Tristan said, licking his lips. "Turn around for me, sweetie, let me taste your pucker. Very well sculpted ass." He kneaded Sebastian's ass cheeks and pulled them apart. Sebastian leaned forward to give him better access and let out a little muffed sound as Tristan's tongue traced the length of his crack and settled over his hole.

From where Alec stood he could see Tristan's tongue flicking inside Sebastian's ass and his cock swelled at the sight. He moved to stand in front of Sebastian to give him some support. Sebastian grasped Alec's hips and leaned over more. "Thank you, Master," he mumbled. His head fell against Alec's stomach with a groan.

Freddie came to join them. Tristan stood and kissed him full on the mouth. "Doesn't he taste wonderful, Freddie?"

"He does. I knew you'd like him."

Tristan coated a finger with spit and pushed into Sebastian, starting a slow, teasing rhythm and turned back to kiss Freddie again.

Sebastian nuzzled his face against Alec's erection. He definitely wanted more, but full sex on the shop floor was probably not the polite thing to do. "Would you like to retire to one of the available rooms for a few minutes, gentlemen?" Alec asked, desperate to get his cock into Sebastian's mouth.

"What a wonderful idea. Come, Freddie, let's play with our new friends."

Maurice opened a door for them as they approached the far end of the shop. The room was dimly lit, but with enough light to make out the action comfortably. In the center stood a fucking horse and a wide leather chaise surrounded by chairs. A long console table occupied one of the long walls. Alec guessed the small silver sachets sitting in two shallow dishes on it contained lube and condoms. A row of coat pegs hung along another wall. The décor was deep red, much like the club. Sebastian knelt at Alec's feet awaiting instruction.

"Are you happy to play or would you like to fuck him?"

"There's an offer I won't pass up. What a darling you are, Alexander. But I should give you something in return. Would you like to fuck my Freddie? He's awfully good."

Alec blinked a few times. Now that was an odd master-boy pairing. "Thank you, that's very kind."

"Wonderful. I'll take the chaise if that's okay. I'll take him on his back. Freddie take off your pants, sweetie and get ready on the horse for Alexander."

"Yes, Tristan." Freddie stood in front of Alec, toed off his shoes and dropped his pants and underwear to the floor. "Do you mind if we kiss first? I like kissing."

"Freddie, don't be so forward. I've told you before, it's the master who has the choices. Now, Sebastian, I like kissing too. May I kiss you and caress you before I slip into that sweet little ass of yours?"

"Master?" Sebastian looked at Alec.

"You may respond as you wish, Sebastian."

"Thank you, Tristan, sir. I like kissing."

Freddie was already leaning over the horse and Alec felt guilty for not responding to his question. His slipped off his clothes and grabbed a couple of sachets of lube and a condom. Fucking without Hamilton's permission again, it seemed odd and yet so right with this new dynamic he had going on with Sebastian. Tristan stripped off only his pants, and crawled over Sebastian where he lay on the chaise.

"Freddie," Alec said, running a hand over the heavily muscled ass. "I'd like to kiss you."

"Thank you, Master Alexander."

The sudden onslaught of making out left Alec a bit dazed. Driven on by Sebastian's delicate moans echoing around the room, Alec felt ready to blow. When Freddie broke away, he looked immediately across at the chaise. "Would you like to sit and watch them first?"

"Can we?"

Alec smiled. "Let's take a seat."

"Oh, do," Tristan chuckled. "With a boy this lovely I'll just be a few minutes." He pulled on a condom and ripped open the packet of lube, coating his cock. "Be honest, Sebastian. You've seen my little cock. Do I need to prep you, or can you take it straight away?"

"It may be tight on the first thrust, sir, but it won't be a problem."

"Good boy. Tell me if it's uncomfortable and I'll stop and open you up first."

"Thank you, sir, for your consideration."

"Such a lovely boy, Alexander. Perfect manners. My Freddie is a wonderful boy too. I like his spirit." With that, Tristan lined up his cock and started to feed it slowly into Sebastian's body. "That is superb. Pop your legs over here, that's it, so your bottom is higher for me."

Freddie started to stroke Alec's cock. They watched Tristan set a steady pace and Sebastian was soon rocking with him. "Can I suck you?" Freddie whispered. Alec nodded and Freddie slipped to his knees and took Alec in fully to the hilt.

"Fucking hell." Alec clenched the arm of a chair and scrunched his eyes tight to stop the orgasm that threatened. He could hear Tristan's airy chuckle. Alec felt completely overwhelmed by the deep throating action. Freddie held his cock in the back of his throat and swallowed the head over and over. He couldn't have been breathing. He released it and let the cock slip out.

"Did you like that?"

"I'll say. I'll fuck you now, while I still have something to give you." Freddie stood to move to the horse. "No, sit on me. That way you can still watch your master."

"Thank you, Master Alexander." Alec pulled on the condom he still had in his hand and lubed his cock. "I don't need you to prep me, sir, unless you'd like to finger me."

"Bend over first, so I can see where I'm going."

Freddie bent forward at the waist and spread his cheeks. His pucker looked enlarged and Alec wondered how often the guy fucked. "Is it to your liking, Master Alexander?"

"Looks good to me, Freddie. On you get." Alec disappeared inside him with hardly any resistance and Freddie started to fuck himself on Alec's cock.

Sebastian had an impressive snail trail of pre-cum over his belly and Tristan looked like he was close. A moment later, the pace faltered and Tristan let out a grunt. He fell forward over Sebastian's chest and started kissing up a storm. "Alexander, can I suck your boy dry?"

Freddie was doing very clever things and Alec found putting words together difficult but he managed a garbled yes. Tristan threw away the condom and dropped his mouth over Sebastian's cock. "Master, Master please," Sebastian called. Alec looked over to see Sebastian reaching for him. *Fuck, fuck, fuck.*

Alec moved Freddie off his lap and knelt at Sebastian's head to stroke his brow. He sat to the side and waved Freddie back onto his cock. Freddie did all the work as Alec concentrated on Sebastian. Alec waited until he was squirming and whimpering, teetering on the edge. "Come for me, Sebastian."

Sebastian arched his back and he grasped Alec's hand. "Yes, Master."

Alec's own orgasm washed over him unexpectedly as Freddie responded to the command and clenched a hand around Alec's cock. Alec squeezed Freddie around the waist. "Thank you, Master Alexander," he panted. "Thank you, Tristan."

"You boys were so much fun," Tristan said. He licked his lips. "And Sebastian has the sweetest cum I've ever tasted."

"Pineapples," Sebastian said, sitting up. "Pineapples, melon and nutmeg… and I eat very little meat. Other than cock." His grin seemed to light up the room.

Tristan and Freddie burst out laughing. "You are delightful. Please say you'll come to the party."

"Not today," Alec said smiling. "But we'll be very interested in your next get together. I'll give you my card."

"Lovely. Come now Freddie. Phillip and Giorgio will have gone on without us."

Sure enough, by the time they dressed Phillip and Giorgio had left and Maurice was with a different customer. A boy sat at his feet.

"Stay in touch." Tristan kissed Alec on both cheeks, stroked Sebastian's hair, and pulled Freddie out of the shop.

"Thank you for being with me," Sebastian said to Alec. "It was our first time and I wanted to do it for you."

"I realized that, after. I'm glad you called for me. You were perfect, such a good boy."

"Thank you, Master. And I love the bracelets."

Maurice smiled at Alec. His expression suggested he had many stories to tell. Alec wondered if one day Maurice would write his memoires. "I'd like you to service Maurice when he's free."

"Thank you, Master."

"Wait for him in the dressing room."

From the corner of his eye Alec saw the man and his boy watch Sebastian head into the back of the store. He figured it wasn't every day you saw a naked man walk past in public. The man said something to Maurice and then looked at Alec. As Maurice glanced up, Alec caught a very subtle shake of his head. *Interesting. Maurice isn't happy with this guy.* The man said something to his boy, who suddenly scurried over to Alec, turned around, dropped his pants, and bent over. He spread his cheeks for Alec's inspection.

"Well?" The man said. "Do you want to fuck him? He's very tight. I popped his cherry just last week and no one else has touched him."

Alec was taken aback by the man' words and his boy's actions. "I don't know what to say." *Other than calling you a complete and total jerk.*

"He needs to be fucked by someone else. I'm taking him to a party tomorrow and he needs to be ready for as many as want to use him."

"I don't mean to question your methods but isn't that a bit soon? Surely the boy needs some training."

"The best way to train them is to fuck them, not mollycoddle them. He's a slave, not a pet."

"Why don't I take him to meet my boy while you're finishing your business with Maurice? Sebastian has been to lots of parties and clubs. He may have some advice for a new boy."

"Excellent. Take him. Fuck him while you're there and have your boy fuck him too."

The poor lad was shaking and Alec touched his shoulder. "You can stand now, pull your pants up."

"Thank you, sir. I want to serve you, sir." It was a good example of what Hamilton had warned him about on the way to his first party. The kid didn't look more than sixteen or seventeen. How the fuck he'd ended up with this monster Alec didn't know, but he was damn sure he wasn't leaving with him.

Alec put an arm around the boy's shoulder and walked him through to the dressing room. "What's your name?"

"I'm not allowed to use my name anymore, sir. I'm Boy."

"This is Sebastian. He's my boy. He has a name and a job and I love him very much. I'm his master and that means I care for him and make sure he's always safe. I'd never leave him with a stranger. In return he serves me."

Sebastian pulled the boy onto a hug. "You poor little thing. How old are you? Tell me the truth; I'll know if you're lying."

"I'm to tell people I'm eighteen…"

As his voice trailed off, Sebastian leaned in close and Alec couldn't make out the whispered words, but he suspected what was said by the angered expression on Sebastian's face.

"Fucking hell, Sebastian. What do we do? Did you hear that guy?"

They kept their voices low as they discussed possibilities. Boy had been sold by his stepfather when he was fourteen. The man he was with had at least waited until legal age before fucking him but intended to use him at clubs and parties. The poor kid wasn't even sure he was gay. His name was Joshua. Alec phoned Hamilton for his advice and Hamilton asked to speak to Joshua's owner.

"Excuse me," Alec said, returning to the store with his phone held out. "I have a colleague, a business associate, who would like to speak to you regarding the boy." Alec handed over the phone and noted the look of relief on Maurice's face as the conversation began and Hamilton's distinct tones filtered through. Alec could pick up the odd word every now and then but still wasn't sure where the conversation was headed. A few minutes later, the man handed the phone back.

"Alec?"

"Yes, it's me."

"Give the man a business card. Under no circumstances do you leave without that boy. You bring him straight to me, do you understand?"

"I understand."

"I'll see you shortly."

Alec ended the call with a smart tap and pulled out a business card. "I believe you're waiting for this."

The man huffed and grabbed the card. Alec fought the urge to take a step back.

"I'll be in touch." He glared at Alec. "Don't even think about ripping me off. I paid good money for that boy." He didn't wait for Alec to respond. He pocketed the business card and marched off.

Maurice let out a breath when the door closed behind the man. "Alec, thank you. The most despicable thing about my job is dealing with men like that."

"He's just a kid, Maurice. He was going to… I can't even think about it."

"It happens too often. Luckily, I don't see many come through here but I know people. I get the kids out when I can. It's awful to say but it's easier when they're younger. The police deal with it. Once they reach the age it's far more complicated."

"I'm taking him to Hamilton's."

"Thank goodness. The man is a saint." Maurice smiled. "But you know that."

"Let me break the good news to Joshua and then I'll be back to settle my bill."

"I'm very pleased to see you connect with Tristan and Freddie by the way. Lovely couple and very respectful. The most wonderful parties. I attend myself sometimes. They worship their boys as though they were angels."

"They were very entertaining. I was going to offer you Sebastian, but I need to get Joshua to Hamilton's before it gets too late. Can we rain check?"

"Why don't you take the boy now and call in next week to settle the bill. I'd like to follow up on the boy myself. You can let me know how he's getting along."

"Then it's a date."

Joshua cried when he realized he'd be going home with them. Genuine tears of relief. He was adamant though, that the man hadn't raped him or beaten him and that other than the ban on using his name, he'd been well cared for. Joshua said the man was even affectionate at times, which was why Joshua agreed to have sex with him. It was just as Hamilton said, a mixed up kid who didn't understand the concept of being a houseboy. Joshua thought it would mean not having to find a job or pay bills and always having somewhere nice to live in return for letting the guy have sex with him occasionally. He hadn't realized he'd be offered up to groups of strangers several times a week.

When they arrived at Hamilton's, two detectives were waiting. They took as many details as the boy knew about his family and the man who'd bought him and interviewed Alec and Sebastian.

"What will happen to him?" Alec asked Hamilton.

"Hopefully he'll go on to live his own life as a free man. I'll do what I can for him. Alec, would you mind if Sebastian stayed here with Joshua until I can place him? I don't want him to be on his own during the day and Sebastian will be able to offer him some support."

"I think Sebastian would like that. But place him where, with a master?"

184

"Heavens no. With a family who can give him the space he needs. Get him an education and let him finish growing up."

"Did I tell you I love you?"

"Not often enough," Hamilton smiled and accepted the kiss Alec offered him. "Stay tonight? The place is so empty without you. My bed is empty without you."

"I'd love to."

Alec watched Sebastian settle Joshua into the guest room with a pair of pajamas, a toothbrush, and orders to take a bath. Sebastian promised to stay with him through the night, just in case he woke up and didn't know where he was.

"You're so good with him, Sebastian."

"He's a sweet kid. I'm glad he's safe. What's Hamilton going to do about the guy?"

"Talk to him, try to explain why there's more benefit in having an older boy who knows he wants to serve and try to coax out of him the contact who put him in touch with the boy's family."

"He thinks it's an organized ring?"

"Maybe just an opportunist. Too early to say. You don't mind looking after Joshua do you?"

"No, I'll stay here with him and do the big-brother thing. We have a lot in common. I hated my stepfather too."

"I don't know anything about you, do I?" A common theme in Alec's new life.

Sebastian kissed him. "You know I'm your boy. What else is there?"

For the first time since they'd been together, Alec shared Hamilton's bed without sex. Instead, the night was full of reassuring touches, warm caresses, and comforting cuddles. They wanted to be close and to remember they were the lucky ones.

Finding a Friend

Everything was backward and Alec wasn't sure how he felt about it. Sebastian was back at Alec's apartment with Joshua because the youngster couldn't settle in Hamilton's posh place. There wasn't enough room for Alec as well, so he stayed with Hamilton. He'd just spent his first weekend without Sebastian in two months and he didn't like it. Hamilton took him and the remaining two boys to the club where Alec saw them in action when they were not imprisoned in a cage. They were impressive. Alec felt quite impressive himself when Hamilton fucked him on a small stage in front of a select audience. He went on to suck a few cocks afterward, but he missed Sebastian's airiness around him to lighten the mood.

Now he stood, staring over the office from his position at the water cooler, wondering what normal life was all about. He was living with the boss. Living with the man who regularly told him to get to his knees and suck strangers' cocks. Not just strangers. Alec had a whole stack of new clients who flopped their dicks out in meetings about their accounts and Alec either swallowed or got covered in their cum. At least he wasn't Michael. Michael's ass was open season. Alec had watched him take one guy after another. It was crazy. But then Michael left it all behind when he went home. For Alec, life had become one long fuckfest.

"Penny for 'em." Tom's hand brushed Alec's ass as he reached for a cup.

"Just pondering the meaning of life, Tom. And are you purposely touching me up or was it a slip of the wrist?"

"Want me to cheer you up on the fourth? I've got a free half hour."

"You're offering to give me a blowjob? I thought you were only for Emma these days."

Tom leaned his chin on Alec's shoulder. "I don't like to see you out of sorts." He took the empty water cup out of Alec's hand. "Come on, if you're quiet you can fuck me too."

Alec let Tom lead him out of the office waiting for him to spring the joke. Fifteen minutes later with his cock pistoning into Tom's body, his hand over Tom's mouth, it sunk in that he'd been serious. "Fuck, Tom, it's damn sexy when you jump me. You're going to be trouble, I can see it."

"Shit." They both stopped, holding their breath when they heard the sound of the door to the bathrooms opening. Alec thanked the building designer for the full, floor to ceiling cubicles.

"Alec, I know you're in here."

"Hey, Michael. What's up?" Alec clapped his hand back over Tom's mouth as he started stuttering a whispered curse.

"I'm guessing you're not alone. Need some help? I can lock this outside door."

Oh, now that's a sexy idea. Michael sucking off Tom as Alec fucked him. Alec reached for the lock on the cubicle door.

"Don't you fucking dare, Caldwell."

"Relax, it'll blow your mind. Coming out Mike. Lock that door." Alec held the condom at the base of his cock and pulled out of Tom.

"I think I hate you, Alec," Tom said, as Alec opened the door and pushed him out into the bathroom.

"Don't be stupid. Tom this is Michael, we fuck quite a bit." Alec gave Michael a quick smooch and noted Tom's deflated cock perk up. "What do you think Michael, does he want to watch me fuck you or shall I finish fucking him?"

Michael slipped to his knees in front of Tom and licked up Tom's shaft. "I'll suck him, you fuck him."

"You're serious?" Tom's voice was no more than a squeak.

"Always," Michael grinned. "Besides, Alec here is needed in the office. So we need to get you finished quickly."

Alec felt the heat drain out of him. "Please tell me Hamilton didn't send you in here."

"Don't waste any more time, Alec." Michael grinned. "It's your ass on the line for being late, not mine."

Alec took a deep breath. He tried to clear the memory of the paddle, his punishment for being late. "I can't do it. Sorry, Tom. I'll never get it up again. Let Michael blow you, he's really good." Alec had the condom off, his pants up and was out of the door before Tom could protest. He didn't even wait for the elevator—took the four flights of stairs and was glad that despite his hectic schedule he still found time for the gym. He was feeling a little sweaty and flushed as he knocked softly on Hamilton's door.

He opened the door at the command and was pissed to see Worthington smiling up at him from the tub chair. *Called away from a decent fuck to suck cock. Damn it.* Hamilton was sitting on the sofa with an amused look on his face. "That was quick."

"I didn't want to keep you waiting, sir."

"I should think not. I wouldn't want to have to punish you in front of Peter."

"No, sir."

"I'll question you on your whereabouts after you've seen to your duties. Lock the door and remove your clothes. Peter will prepare you to be fucked and you can service him."

Alec stalled. *Prepare him to be fucked... by Worthington?* He made it to the door but as his mind registered the lock clicking into place his body froze. No. He couldn't do it. He *wouldn't* do it. He should be fucking Tom on the fourth floor not being fucked by some old man with a fat dick. Shit, what was he going to do? Walk out. He should just walk out of the office and go home. But he couldn't go home. He didn't have anywhere to get away from this stupid, crazy, fucking nightmare job that left him without a moment to himself. He jumped as a hand touched his arm.

"Are you okay, Alec?" Worthington looked worried as Alec turned to face him. "I'll come back another time. You don't look well. You're very pale."

"I… I'm sorry, sir. I'm fine really. I…" But he wasn't fine. He swayed on his feet, the walls started to move in on him, and a wave of nausea washed over him. He dashed to Hamilton's private bathroom and emptied the contents of his stomach into the toilet bowl. He let his body slump to the tiles. Definitely too heavy to move and his eyes wouldn't open.

Something cold and damp pressed against his head but he couldn't bring himself to see who or what. Voices murmured around him. He didn't want to know what they were saying. *Strip him and fuck him while he can't fight.* His eyes snapped open. Just his mind playing tricks.

Hamilton and Worthington helped him to his feet, debating whether to call a doctor or just let him sleep on the couch for a while.

"I'm sorry," he managed to squeak, but Hamilton wasn't taking any notice. Instead, he handed Alec a glass of water and a tablet and watched him take it. He took off Alec's shoes and laid him out on the sofa with a kiss to the temple. Alec closed his eyes for just a moment…

Alec opened his eyes. The office was dark. He was snuggled under a soft, blanket wrapped around him and for a moment couldn't re-member why he was lying on Hamilton's sofa.

"How are you feeling?"

Alec twisted his head to see Hamilton seated at his desk, his face barely illuminated by the glow from his laptop.

"What time is it?"

"Nearly nine. You've been asleep most of the day."

"Crap." Alec sat up. He didn't feel lightheaded so swung his feet around. "I'm really sorry, Rick. I don't know what happened."

"I do. I've been over taxing you. I underestimated the gravity of your lifestyle change, thought because you were young you'd handle it."

"I am handling it."

"Maybe you've taken on too much."

"No, Rick, please don't. I like my life. I love my life. I love you, I just… I miss Sebastian, I got stressed about being late for you and…"

"And you'd rather have been fucking Tom than servicing Peter for me."

"No, that's not it. I… I just lost myself for a moment."

Hamilton stood and walked around the desk. He sat next to Alec and put an arm around him. "I'm very fond of you, Alec. But you have to understand I'm not very good at sensing people's needs. If you need a break, you have to tell me. I've never looked after someone so completely new to the life before. I can't even begin to imagine what it must be like for you."

"I was scared. It's stupid. I thought Peter was going to fuck me. My brain disconnected."

"Alec, how many times do I have to tell you I won't hand you out? Don't you trust me?"

"Of course I do, I told you it was stupid."

Hamilton chuckled. "Are you ready to go home? I'll have Sebastian come over if you like, leave the two of you alone for a while."

As much as Alec wanted it, he had the feeling Hamilton would be upset if Alec agreed. And besides, Alec really was happy, wasn't he? "You're all I need, Rick. I'm okay now. It was just a wobble."

"As long as you're sure. I don't want you stressed unnecessarily."

"How long do you think Joshua will be around? I don't want to throw the kid out or anything, but it'll help me pace myself."

"He'll be gone by the weekend. I've found a family for him in Winchester. He'll get the best care and the best education."

"They won't mess with him?"

"He'll be perfectly safe and free to grow up as nature intended, however that happens to be."

"Any news from the police?"

"Nothing of any significance. The guy was an opportunist. Nothing they can build a case with but they'll keep an eye on him for a while. Come on, let's go home. We can pick up some food on the way."

Hamilton watched Alec like a hawk for the next few days. Every time Alec turned around he caught a glimpse of Hamilton hovering. It was reassuring and unnerving at the same time. Was he watching to make sure Alec was okay or that he wasn't running off with Tom for a quick screw? It was difficult to tell. At least Alec hadn't been called in to service anyone. In a strange way he missed it. It was part of his daily routine now—sucking rich men's cocks. Not doing it left him feeling as though he'd forgotten something important. Alec shuffled his paperwork and tidied his desk ready to leave for the evening. He was starting to feel like a spare part. Perhaps he could persuade Hamilton to let him give someone a blowjob before they went home.

He knocked on Hamilton's door and opened it without waiting. It was a good job he closed it behind him before looking properly. As the reality of what he saw filtered through, he froze. It wasn't as though Alec didn't know Hamilton fucked other people. Hell, Alec fucked other people. But the sight of Hamilton buried balls deep in Tom's body was still a shock.

"What the fuck is going on?"

Hamilton smoothed a hand over Tom's back, just as he usually did with Alec, and a spike of jealousy stabbed through Alec's mind and left a crushing sensation in his chest.

"I thought I'd see what keeps you going back for more." Hamilton smiled but it didn't reach his eyes. "He's a nice, tight fuck. I can see why you like him."

"You selfish, rotten, bastard. You had to, didn't you? You had to take the one thing that was just mine."

"Alec." Tom reached out for him, but Hamilton grabbed his hand and trapped it behind Tom's back.

"You can fuck off too. I thought you were my friend. Fuck the boss behind my back is it? Tell me I'm your only one. Fucker."

Alec was out of the office and in the elevator before he could take a breath without snorting fire. Tom was his, he wasn't an office boy, he wasn't part of the Order and he knew… Tom knew how much Alec fancied Hamilton. Why would he fuck him? Alec felt the world spinning out of control. He wanted to kick and scream and shout, throw things, break stuff, but he couldn't. He couldn't even go home.

He headed for the tube station and got on the first train, not even looking at where it was headed. Ah, the Circle Line, at least he wouldn't end up too far out of his way. But his way to where? Why was everything so fucked up all of a sudden? At least on the tube he was safe from texts and phone calls. Alec decided he'd rather not know whether Hamilton and Tom were trying to get hold of him. He didn't want to know if they cared enough to be concerned about hurting him. But he couldn't ride the Underground all evening.

Alec got off at the next stop—Victoria. It was so tempting to buy a train ticket and disappear but instead he grabbed a coffee, a cinnamon bun, and a seat in a corner of the cafe. Maybe he'd call Sebastian and get him to come out and meet him. But there was no way Sebastian would leave Joshua and Alec couldn't face the kid right now.

Alec didn't know anyone else. Before Hamilton it would have been Tom he called. He had Peter Worthington's number, but the man probably had a family and would want a blowjob. Maurice was out of the question—a sex shop was the last place Alec wanted to be. Michael was a possible, but Alec would have to call Hamilton for his number. He flicked through his billfold and the pile of business cards, most of which were his new cocksucker clients, and found a saving grace—Tristan. The guy had seemed nice, perhaps he'd come out for a drink.

"Tristan speaking."

Alec felt a flush of relief wash over him. "Hi, it's Alexander, we met last week."

"Oh how lovely. I'm afraid there are no parties this weekend, but you're welcome to come and visit for nibbles."

"Actually, Tristan, I've had a bit of a godawful shit day and was wondering if you fancied getting together this evening?"

"Sweetie, you come straight here. I'll have Freddie cook something wonderful and we can set the world to rights."

"Is this your address on the business card you gave me?"

"Yes, darling. I'll see you soon."

As soon as Alec rang off his phone chirped its happy tune. It was Hamilton. Alec sent the call to voicemail. He had a missed call from Tom and a text. "So sorry mate, I couldn't say no. Forgive me?"

Alec ignored all three. He headed back down to the tube in the direction of Kensington. With any luck he'd fuck Freddie, maybe Tristan too. The way he was feeling, he'd likely let Tristan and Freddie fuck him as well. Another cock up his ass could be just what Alec needed to shake free of the hold Hamilton had over him. Fucking on the rebound was probably not the best idea, but with enough wine down his throat Alec hoped the alcohol buzz would remove the decision-making process and let nature take its course.

By the time Alec surfaced in South Kensington he had another three missed calls from Hamilton and one curt text—*Alec, you will contact me immediately.* Alec flopped down on the nearest bench. Why was it such a fight not to follow orders? His fingers hovered over the call button on his phone. Tristan was waiting. Alec wasn't going to go back to Hamilton's, he needed a break and yet, he couldn't ignore that text. He couldn't. It didn't say to call it just said contact. Alec tapped out a text, *Visiting friends for the evening*, but he didn't send it. Instead, he hit the call button.

"Where in the blazes are you? And how dare you insult me and walk out."

"Rick, I'm not going to argue with you. I'm not coming back."

There was a brief pause. A ripple of unease ran through Alec as he realized what he'd said. But Hamilton wouldn't take him literally would he? Wouldn't think Alec was breaking up with him for good?

"What are you talking about? Alec, where are you? I'll pick you up in the car."

"You have no idea how much you've hurt me, do you? I'm on my way to a friend's."

"Alec, help me out here. Tell me what you need."

"I need you to understand how much I love you and how seeing you fuck my best friend ripped a hole in my chest that's going to take time to heal."

"You're serious?"

Alec hung up. No point being honest if all Hamilton could do was make fun of him. He was still sitting on the bench when a text came through. *Please let me make things right. Don't let me lose you, Alec. Come home.*

Alec tapped out the reply. *I need time to get my head around why you can't see things the way I do.* He started the walk to Tristan's.

Another text beeped but Alec didn't look at it. For once, Hamilton would have to wait.

Tristan fussed and flounced over Alec. It was easy company and Alec poured out his troubled heart to the gasps and shrieks of his new friend while Freddie cooked. The wine flowed, the food was great, and neither of them laid a finger on Alec other than to offer a shoulder to cry on. It was a relief to have something stay outside of the realms of sex. Now all Alec had to do was decide whether to stay over.

"You know you're welcome, darling." Tristan said, squeezing Alec's shoulder. "You can have the spare room or cuddle up for some TLC."

"What do you think I should do, Tristan?"

"Honestly? I think you should go home. Never go to bed with bad blood between you, my mother always told me. If you love him, Alec, however much of a bastard you think he's been, you have to go to him and give him the chance to put it right."

"Why are you so kind to me?"

"Because you have a good heart," Tristan said. He pressed his finger to the end of Alec's nose. "I knew it from the very first moment. Only the very best fuck my Freddie, he's far too precious to share with just anyone."

Alec managed a smile. "Time I left you and Freddie some space of your own then."

"Call him, Alec. Ask him to pick you up from here. Let him see you have friends who are willing to support you."

"Thank you. It means a lot to me. I felt so lost earlier but I'm stronger now."

"Good boy." Tristan kissed Alec's forehead and handed him the phone. "You still have the address?"

Alec nodded and dialed the number. Hamilton picked up on the first ring.

"Alec? I've been so worried. Why didn't you answer any more of my calls or texts?"

"Come and get me, Rick?" Alec gave him the address and sat back to wait for the next round. Would Hamilton punish him for being so difficult? Probably. But things had settled out in Alec's mind. He was determined to try and see things from Hamilton's view. Tom was another matter altogether. "I couldn't say no, mate," didn't really cut it, but Hamilton lived one of the most fucked-up lives Alec had ever encountered. Perhaps he deserved a little slack. Alec figured he'd know how much slack he was willing to give as soon as Hamilton showed up. Until then, he was going to kick back and relax with his new friends, happy in the knowledge he finally had somewhere to go when things got tough.

Clearing the Path

Chloe was being a pain. She insisted on forcing conversation between Alec and Tom, and really pushed for the details of what was wrong with the pair of them.

Alec slammed a folder on his desk. "Give it a rest, will you!"

"No. We've been friends for years, Alec. Shared this cubicle for too long for me to ignore what's going on here. You can't make me work in Siberia and, believe me, that's what it feels like right now. Sort it out."

Alec looked at Tom's hopeful face, the tentative smile, and wanted to punch him. "I'm late for a meeting." Alec gathered his stuff and marched off to Hamilton's office. Before he could close the door, Tom slipped in behind him.

"Sorry, Mr. Hamilton," Tom said, pushing Alec to one side against the wall. "Alec, you can't just ignore me. I've said I'm sorry a hundred times."

Hamilton walked over and stroked Alec's cheek. "I'll leave you two together for a few minutes. Do the right thing, Alec." Alec closed his eyes at the tender kiss Hamilton placed on his cheek. He was cheating. Hamilton knew Alec couldn't help but do everything he suggested. Their own reunion had been heated and passionate. There was shouting and rough hands and Freddie standing between them to prevent violence but it soon toppled over into the clashing of bodies with very different expressions. A desperate need to fit together, to caress and heal and fuck out the pain they'd inflicted on each other.

Once at home, Alec took his punishment for not doing as he was told. His ass stung for days but he understood the need for it. His storming off without listening interrupted Hamilton's plan for a threesome. He'd only been testing the water with Tom to get a feel for how it might work one evening at his home. The punishment also reestablished the necessary boundaries. Alec liked his boundaries, craved them in fact. The new closeness between Alec and Hamilton now they'd made up, didn't extend to Tom. Alec had a mental block when it came to forgiving him.

So now what? Tom still held Alec against the wall as Hamilton closed the door behind him. "Please, Alec. Just talk to me. Shout, scream, slap me if you have to but don't shut me out. I can't stand it anymore."

"You should have thought about that before you fucked my boyfriend."

Tom sighed and let go of Alec's arm. "You told me you were living with a guy called Sebastian. How was I supposed to know you were doing the boss as well?"

"Fine, but you knew how much I wanted him. I guess you had to go there first, is that it?"

"Why are you so mad with me and yet you've let him off without a second thought? Did he tell you what happened, did you even damn well ask him?"

Alec took a moment to gather his thoughts. He hadn't asked Hamilton how it happened, just why. He wasn't stupid enough to think Tom had made the first move. "Tell me, then. Tell me your side of it."

"I wish I knew what to say. I'm still not sure how I ended up with my pants down if I'm honest. One minute I was chatting about you, the next he was fucking me. Other than a few hand strokes in between, I don't really understand how we got from one stage to the next."

That sounded about right. Alec remembered feeling like that after fucking Michael the first time. Hamilton had a way of orchestrating a flow of events so smoothly it was happening before your brain caught up with where things were heading.

"What were you saying about me?"

"He asked me about us, if I liked you. I got carried away, Alec. I didn't want to steal your bloke or get there first. He hit on me. I was wrong not to stop it, I know that, but if you can let him off, surely you can give me another chance?" Tom pressed Alec against the wall and leaned into his ear. "Please, Alec. I miss you."

"It's not about second chances, Tom. I keep seeing the two of you together in my head. It makes me angry."

"But only with me, I suppose."

"I've watched him fuck loads of people. But up until then, you were just mine."

"So that's it then? I fucked the boss and now I have to transfer because you can't work with me anymore?"

Alec let out a deep breath. The times he'd thought it was going to be Tom who made life at work difficult and yet there he was forcing the guy out of the department. Alec let his head fall on Tom's shoulder. "I don't want you to leave, idiot. Just let me be mad at you for a while."

Tom kissed his neck and face. "I hate seeing you like this. I'll never let him touch me again, I promise, and I am yours, whenever you want me."

Alec let himself melt into Tom's embrace. As much as he wanted to be mad at him, he couldn't, not when he was hurting so much. "You don't have to do that."

"Alec, I really like you. I like having sex with you."

"I mean you don't have to stay away from him. I'm over it now, it happened. If you want to do it again, do it."

"But I thought you two were an item?"

"We are. But like I said, I've seen him fuck loads of guys, including my Sebastian. I'm not mad that he was fucking behind my back or that you were. It was just the cross-over that grated. You were the one person who was just mine. Everyone else I've fucked, he's fucked too." *Hmm, not strictly true, there is Freddie.*

"Alec, I really am sorry." Tom began to stroke Alec's shoulder. "Why are you with him if it upsets you?"

"It doesn't usually. I guess I like you more than I realized. The way I'm feeling, it's more to do with you than with Hamilton, and I'm sorry for that. I didn't mean for this to turn into a gushy teenage crush."

Tom chuckled. "Is that what it is? You've got a crush on me? Well, I'm man enough to say I love you, Alec Caldwell. In a grown up, 'you're a good mate and I love it when you fuck me' way, rather than 'I want to have your babies and be with you forever' way."

Alec reached for Tom's lips and savored the sweet taste of his words. "I love you too, stupid."

Life settled back to normal. As normal as Alec could call his life. Joshua was settling in with his new family in Winchester, Alec was back at home with Sebastian, and Tom was… just Tom. Alec resumed his full Order duties and Hamilton was being especially attentive to his needs. But there were a couple of things outstanding. Alec wanted to take Sebastian to one of Tristan's parties and to Maurice for the servicing he'd promised the shop-keeper. Sebastian didn't know it yet, but tonight was shopping night. Alec had ideas about a few things he'd like to try. In their time together, Alec had discovered Sebastian had a thing for being restrained. It was something Alec definitely wanted to explore.

A naked Sebastian wrapped himself around Alec no sooner than he closed the front door. "Master." He slid down Alec's body and kissed his crotch. "Can I service you before dinner?"

So tempting. Alec stroked his hair. "Not tonight, sweetheart. I'm taking you out. We owe a little something to our friend, Maurice, and…" Alec said, fingering Sebastian's bands, "…I want to find some cuffs that will work with these."

Only the mischief in his eyes outshone the light in Sebastian's smile . "Thank you, Master."

Dinner was a speedy affair, and a quick tube train ride later they entered the emporium with the familiar tinkle of the door bell.

"Alec, how lovely."

"Maurice, I'm sorry it's taken so long. Sebastian is at your service, if you have a moment."

"I do have some time. What are you offering?"

Alec looked at Sebastian with a smile. "I'd like to find some good strong cuffs that won't rub with his bracelets. Once we have them, I'll strap him down and you can fuck him, if you'd like."

Alec noted Maurice's shudder. "I have just the thing," he said, his voice on the throaty side. Within ten minutes Maurice was pounding into Sebastian. He looked so sexy trussed up with his arms raised behind his back and attached by chains to a hook in the ceiling. Ankle cuffs strapped to a spreader bar presented his ass at the perfect angle for fucking. It was apparent from the flush on Sebastian's cheeks that he was only just getting started when Maurice grunted and came. Alec left Sebastian in position as Maurice cleaned up and went through into the main shop. When he unlocked the door a rowdy bunch of guys poured in.

"Fucking hell, look at that," one of them said, pointing at Sebastian in the back room.

Maurice hustled them out of the shop until only two remained. He gave Alec an apologetic glance, but Alec already had other ideas. He left the door to the private room open, with Sebastian still on show, and started browsing the racks of dildos.

"Is he yours?"

Alec turned to meet dark brown eyes, framed by long dark lashes. The man was breathtaking. Smooth, cocoa skin, cropped hair, and the tightest tee-shirt and jeans Alec had seen in a long while. "Yes, mine."

"He's beautiful."

"Thank you."

"I'm Marcus, this is my partner Kyle."

Kyle was just as perfect. Hair a little longer, eyes more hazel than brown, skin a shade or two lighter, but he was exquisite. Every muscle was well defined and wrapped in clinging clothes that showed every curve.

"It's nice to meet you. I'm Alexander, my boy is Sebastian."

"Your boy?"

"Sebastian is my slave."

Kyle squeezed Marcus's hand. "Ask him."

"Kyle, stop it."

"Ask me what?"

"Kyle's just being silly."

"Marcus, please ask him."

"I'm happy for you to ask me anything, really," Alec said, intrigued by Kyle's insistence.

"Kyle is a slave, my slave, or at least we're working on it. We're new to the scene. He's always pushing me to ask how it works for other people."

"Shall I bring you some coffee?" Maurice piped up from the counter.

"Thank you, Maurice. Do you mind if we continue using the room?"

"You're very welcome, sir."

Alec motioned to the open doorway. From the upturned angle of his cock, Sebastian was very interested in the turn of the conversation.

"Shall we?" Alec invited.

Kyle walked around Sebastian. He ran his fingers over the hook and chains that held Sebastian in position.

"You can touch him, if you want to," Alec said. He stroked Sebastian's ass.

Kyle looked at Marcus, who nodded his approval and Kyle immediately took hold of Sebastian's cock and gave it several firm strokes.

"So how does it work for you?" Marcus asked.

"Sebastian does whatever I tell him to."

"During sex?"

"For everything."

"It's not just a bedroom game?"

"Not for us. It's more of a lifestyle. I own him, look after him, and he lives in service to me."

"That's what Kyle says he wants, but I don't think he knows what it means."

Kyle let go of Sebastian and looked up. "I do," he said.

"Okay then, Kyle. Show me you mean it. Take off your clothes."

Kyle stripped and stood before Marcus with his hands covering his erection. "Master, I am yours to do with as you will." The look in Kyle's eye when he met Alec's gaze was nothing short of hungry.

"You're not going to fuck him, Kyle."

Kyle pouted and Alec felt a bit lost with what was going on between the two men. It seemed Kyle didn't have much idea of who was in control. "I'd like to offer you Sebastian, Marcus."

"I'm sorry?"

Alec elaborated. "You can fuck him."

"I haven't even spoken to him."

"You don't need to. He's my slave. If I say you can fuck him, he'll bend over and take you. Of course he's already presented and lubed. He's already been fucked once since we've been here."

"You just offer him out and he doesn't mind?"

"He likes to serve me and if that means being fucked, so be it."

"Okay. I'll fuck him and you can fuck Kyle."

It seemed to be a challenge thrown down to Kyle and Alec wondered if he should step away from the situation, but Kyle handed Alec a condom and a sachet of lube and leaned over the back of the chair beside Sebastian. Alec let autopilot take over. Kyle came before he did and squirmed when Alec didn't stop. "Is there a problem Kyle?"

"No, feels good."

"Master." Alec turned at Sebastian's whimper. Marcus had finished fucking and was giving Sebastian some very vigorous deep-throat action. The sight tipped Alec over the edge, the familiar rush swept through him and he held Kyle's hips fast as he emptied into the condom. To help his thoughts settle down, he admired with his hands the smooth curve of Kyle's deliciously muscled ass cheeks.

"Is he okay?" Kyle asked. Sebastian was making a sweet little keening noise that made Alec smile.

"He's more than okay but he won't come without my permission."

"Seriously?"

"A slave never does anything without permission, Kyle," Alec said, watching closely for his reaction. The shock was apparent.

"Are you going to let him come?"

"Not yet. I'm going to plug him and take him to a friend's house. Once they've fucked him, I'll fuck him myself and he'll come with me."

Marcus stopped his tongue action and looked over. "You don't want me to finish him?"

"No. But you can carry on playing with him. I'm going to find a good size plug. I'll be back in a moment." Alec left the room, still naked. Ignoring the people in the shop, he browsed for a butt plug.

"Well, well, if it isn't Hamilton's boy."

Alec swirled around. *Shit, of all people.* Alec felt a sick feeling in his stomach as Miles Henry's eyes raked over his body. He wasn't alone. A giant ape of a man stood just behind. Alec stepped back as Henry made a beeline for him. Alec looked to Maurice for help, but he was busy with a customer. The next thing he knew, the gorilla bundled Alec into an empty room. Henry followed and closed the door. His man took up a stance against it to block any hope of escape.

Henry smirked. "You caused me a lot of trouble with your little story. I had to pay a large fine to the Order. I think I deserve some compensation from you, Alec."

"Absolutely not. My decision now is the same as before and if you push it I will report you again."

Henry swooped on Alec and pinned him against the wall with one hand while the other went straight for his cock. "Come now, what's a few fingers between friends?" Henry's hand slipped between Alec's legs, squeezing past his balls and slipping over the dam to stroke Alec's pucker. "You're so sexy. Alec. I'll make it good for you." Henry increased the pressure of the two fingers against Alec's hole. "Won't you let me in?"

Alec took a deep breath. "I said, no. Get your hands *off* me."

Henry let go and stepped away. "What a shame. I could have Brian hold you down. You're in a locked room with me and naked, who would believe it was against your will?"

"Hamilton and Harrison for starters, and most people who know me. I have another matter to attend to next door. If you'll excuse me." Alec squared his shoulders to the gorilla and was surprised when Brian stepped aside. Neither man prevented him unlocking the door and leaving. He returned to the other room and unhooked Sebastian.

"Master, what's wrong?"

"Time for us to leave. Unwanted company."

Marcus looked concerned. "Have we overstayed our welcome?"

"No, Marcus. Forgive me. We have to go." Alec pulled on his clothes. "Take my card. Call me. We often go to clubs and parties, maybe we could get together again."

"I'd love to fuck Sebastian some more."

"Okay. Call me and we'll arrange something."

Marcus touched a hand to Alec's arm. "Tell me, Alec, what kind of master wears slave-bands of his own?"

Alec reached for his collar. After his run in with Henry, it gave him comfort to feel it there. Indirectly it had given him the strength to say no. "A subject for another time. Are you ready, Sebastian?"

"Yes, Master, thank you."

"Sebastian?" Marcus reached for Sebastian's shoulder and Alec bristled. Sebastian looked at Alec.

"You may speak to him."

"Yes, sir?" Sebastian said, turning back to look up at Marcus.

"Would you like me to fuck you again?"

"If Master wishes it."

"But what about you, and what you want?"

"I want only to serve Master."

Alec took Sebastian's hand and swept out of the private room without waiting for Marcus's response.

Henry was still browsing out in the main shop but he didn't say anything else. He watched as Alec settled his bill. Alec could still feel Henry's hand around his cock and he shuddered uncomfortably. He was in two minds whether to skip Tristan's and just go home, but after Henry's attempted assault, Tristan and Freddie would be a welcome distraction. And besides, Sebastian had a lot of catching up to do with his fuck rota. The poor guy had been celibate looking after Joshua, hadn't even jerked off. The evening's fuckfest was Alec's way of thanking him for staying faithful.

It was oddly relaxing to sit back and watch one cock after another slip into Sebastian's ass, possibly, because Sebastian was obviously enjoying it so much. Alec fucked a couple of the boys at the party without climaxing—he wanted to save himself for Sebastian's finale. In a quiet moment in the bathroom, he swapped a few sucks and a fingering with Tristan. It was deeply erotic and emotionally intense. Tristan had magic fingers and a very sexy kiss that made Alec wonder what it would be like to be fucked by someone else. He'd come close once with Wessex, but with Tristan, Alec felt the tug in his gut. He wanted to let Tristan fuck him, even though he couldn't find the courage to follow through.

Things were definitely changing. A few weeks ago, Alec would never have considered letting anyone but Hamilton take his ass. Alec didn't know if it was because of what had happened with Tom, but new feelings now stirred in the pit of his stomach. Hot, rampant feelings, which only ever seemed dampened by his on-going fuckfest of a life, yet never fully quenched.

The thoughts dissipated in the moment that Sebastian's ass tightened around Alec's cock and pulled the climax from his body with a deep, throaty cry. All that remained was the need to hold Sebastian close, the sweat from their bodies mingling, his eyelids heavy with the post-orgasmic haze. Some things may change, but the freedom Alec had found with Sebastian, would always be the same.

And thus ends Volume One of The Erotic Adventures of Alec Caldwell, a young London businessman inducted into the exclusive Order of Gentleman.